When Rallus quits his FBI job and moves to the mountain town of Fawnskin, California, to get away from it all, he has no clue that rural life will mean falling in love with another mysterious newcomer. He falls hard and fast for Knox Baylor, who's taken an unusual job as a shomerim, a corpse watcher at a funeral home.

For Knox, the job should be easy money, even if the hours are long . . .except that he falls asleep on the job and accidentally releases Mr. Harold Hoxheimer's angry spirit, or dybbuk, which starts creating unholy havoc in Fawnskin.

Harold opens all the secret wounds festering under Fawnskin's pretty, postcard exterior. Fawnskin is home to a fake fortune teller who blackmails residents but hides an even more sinister secret. And why do individuals keep dying in the old people's home? Rallus barely has time to deal with these problems when a grizzly murder takes place and a small boy is abducted.

As they investigate, Rallus and Knox find that nothing is what it seems in this once-quiet town with the warm and fuzzy name . . .everybody has a secret, and some are willing to go to deadly lengths to keep them.

How can they keep Mr. Hoxheimer's vengeful dybbuk from jumping from one host body to the next? What exactly does he want? And can Rallus and Knox defeat the growing evil with true love?

This book has been previously published and re-released.

Fawnskin
Copyright © 2018 A.J. Llewellyn and D.J. Manly
ISBN: 978-1-4874-2231-8
Cover art by Martine Jardin

Published by eXtasy Books Inc or
Devine Destinies, an imprint of eXtasy Books Inc

Look for us online at:
www.eXtasybooks.com or www.devinedestinies.com

FAWNSKIN
FAWNSKIN BOOK 1

BY

A.J. LLEWELLYN AND D.J. MANLY

DEDICATION

A. J. and D. J. would like to dedicate this book to their readers, with love

CHAPTER ONE

He could see snow falling outside. It was a wonderful, hypnotic image against the rush of Mrs. King's voice.

"You cannot fall asleep. It's imperative you understand that."

The woman sitting opposite Knox Baylor looked calm and had a small, half-smile on her face, but his gaze traveled to her hands frantically shredding their third tissue in as many minutes. Man, she was a bundle of nerves.

"This is a very orthodox Jewish family, and they take shomerim, the guardians of the dead, very much to heart." Mrs. King shifted in her seat and reached down, tugging her skirt toward her knees again, sending wisps of white to the floor. She plucked another tissue out of the box and once again wound it into a knot and began ripping it.

"It's very important to them that Mr. Herxheimer's soul is protected at all costs."

Knox wasn't sure if she was joking, but he wasn't. Eighty-one whole miles he'd driven from Los Angeles, and he needed this job. He'd read the ad in the Daily News a couple of times and called as soon as the funeral home opened at nine o'clock. By then, he'd joined the morning peak-hour throng of traffic, only he drove against it. As everybody else left the fashionable mountain city of Big Bear, a couple of hours north of LA, he headed straight to it. His gas gauge had hit empty two miles on the long, uphill climb to the town of Fawnskin.

"I understand," he said.

1

He liked the soothing, warm beige tones to the room. Outside a big picture window looking onto the mountains, snowflakes fell from the sky, and he tried not to ogle. He'd lived in California all his life but had never seen snow. And here it was, not even two hours out of Los Angeles.

On the wall above a fireplace, a homey Thomas Kinkade painting of a family strolling by a river, done in the Impressionist style, conveyed the feeling of life going on. He could have studied the painting longer, but Mrs. King's agitation, at odds with her cheery, if bizarre appearance, kept his interest. A large German woman with a massive blonde beehive hairdo, Mrs. King seemed to smile out of habit, even as her eyes registered total terror. She's afraid, he realized as she ran right over his response.

She plucked yet another tissue from the box. "You needn't worry about Mr. Herxheimer's body."

"I won't." I think.

Bits of tissue fell around her feet as she tugged at her hemline again. His gaze fell on her feet. She wore unattractive ankle boots, which only accentuated her thick ankles and legs.

"We have him covered with a cloth . . . a linen cloth." Her head inclined and he gathered this was an important fact, though he had no idea why.

She smelled of a faint rose perfume and mint toothpaste. It was a comforting mix of scents.

"In the Jewish faith, everything from the cloth to the pine box must be biodegradable. I want to make sure you're okay about sitting with the dead . . . with Mr. Herxheimer laid out on the floor beside you."

Knox gave her what he hoped was a reassuring smile. "Absolutely. Not a problem."

"The body . . . Mr. Herxheimer . . . is never left alone for a minute."

He nodded. She'd already repeated this point several times.

Even as he'd idled outside the Lakeside Funeral Home on North Shore Drive, he hadn't thought twice about applying for the job. The thought that it might be a joke only occurred to him in this moment.

Now, as he sat here thinking, I'm having a Six Feet Under moment, he listened to the facts. As creepy as it sounded, he wasn't backing out. He needed this job so badly he wanted to scream. He needed the money. A hundred and fifty dollars sure beat . . . what he'd been doing up until now.

Knox wondered if it was rude to ask for more coffee. He'd left the warm confines of LA and hadn't realized snow was coming into the tiny town of Fawnskin so soon.

He was freezing.

"I'm more than up to the task." He licked his lips, picking up his cup. Not a dreg, nothing.

"More coffee?" she asked.

"I would love it." It had been two days since he'd eaten and scraped enough pennies to buy gas for the drive. By some miracle, his cell phone hadn't been cut off yet, and he'd been able to call, indicating his interest.

Mrs. King was very nice, very comforting in her bosomy, mothering way, even if he didn't get the whole sitting with the dead thing. He knew the body was in the next room. She'd already told him that. He felt a slight shiver. Somebody was sitting with it now, and he would take over if he got the job. He couldn't get back to LA without it. He had to get it. He anticipated a long afternoon and evening of sleeping in his car trying to figure out how to get back home if things didn't pan out.

Oh man . . . it's snowing hard now. I don't have tire chains . . . aren't I supposed to get tire chains in this weather?

Babysitting a corpse in a funeral parlor sounded a whole lot better than freezing his ass off in the damned car that he'd been living in for the last two months.

He followed her to the kitchen, which to his surprise was warm and cheery, even if a little overloaded with a red-heart motif. The hot coffee smell reached his nose, and he had to fight his urge to salivate at the sight of cooling muffins in a cupcake pan.

"Help yourself," she said, and he snatched out his hand hoping he could eat it without appearing to inhale it whole.

Mrs. King retrieved milk from the fridge.

"You will sit with Mr. Herxheimer, from ten o'clock to-night until ten o'clock tomorrow morning. My son normally does it but he and his wife just had a baby, and he's tired. So you see, you cannot fall asleep. You do understand that, right?"

"Yes," he said. You will sit . . . that means I have the job, right? He was so thrilled to receive a second cup of coffee, he might have agreed to a kidney extraction.

"You like my muffins? Here, have a cookie. They're ko-sher."

She opened a large white box with a foil label reading Parker's Crazy Cookies. He stared at the array of peculiar little people cut into cookie shapes. There was a chubby man with an egg-shaped head and big glasses, a couple of other people who were skinnier, making for smaller cookies. He selected a rotund woman-cookie with big hair. He bit into it. Not bad at all. He felt the weight of Mrs. King's stare and guessed these were expensive cookies.

Mrs. King pointed to one of the egg-shaped head cookies. "That's Mr. Herxheimer."

"Excuse me?"

"These were custom-made by his loving family. You just ate his wife."

Knox was stunned. "Well, um . . . she was um . . . sweet and um . . . just a little bit spicy."

Mrs. King snorted with laughter. "Have another one."

He selected a skinny cookie. It was a woman in overalls and a David Cassidy haircut. Lesbian, was his first thought.

The cookies were so good, yet so tiny, he took another. Mrs. King smiled. Maybe she was used to guys loading up on her funeral parlor cookies.

"Now," she said, pushing the box away firmly, "you can work on your laptop, you can read, listen to music, on your earphones only . . . I don't mind, but you can't fall asleep."

He yearned to snatch another muffin. His stomach screamed for more food. Man, I can't stop myself . . . eat this cookie slowly, kid.

"What happens if I fall asleep?" he asked and regretted it when he saw two red spots appear on her waxy, chubby cheeks.

"The spirit of the dead body wanders and becomes a dybbuk."

The remaining cookie crumbled all over his chin and clothing. He hastened to clean it up.

"A dybbuk?"

She nodded. "A malicious spirit."

Mrs. King said this in a matter of fact way. He stared at her in shock. Did she really believe this?

"Oh, yes. It's a very big deal. The spirit wanders and attaches itself to a living person, a kind of host body. This is one of the reasons the body is never left alone. Not for a single minute."

She topped off his coffee. "Many Jewish families believe this and well . . ." Her voice faltered. "They are usually busy sitting shiva, you know, sitting with the living relatives, so they are pleased to pay a stranger to help."

Mrs. King put the coffee pot back on its hot plate.

"With the summer camps, the paper mill and so many other businesses closing here, we've been able to run our business pretty much on our own. Now a new retirement community has opened up . . . and frankly" — her voice dropped — "a lot of them are Jewish, and er . . . elderly if you get my drift, I find we need more help."

"I see." Does she believe this wandering spirit nonsense?

"If this works out, you could earn a nice little sum of money with us," she said. "My son wants to leave a little before nine tonight. Can you be here by eight forty-five?"

"Sure."

"You drove from the city, didn't you?"

"Yes."

She sighed. "I know times are tough. You're the second person who answered our ad. The first one was a local, but I wasn't comfortable leaving Mr. Herxheimer's body in his care. He was a little too . . ." She scrunched her nose and seemed to change her mind about what she was going to say.

He was anxious to know how the local displeased her, but she went on.

"Anyway, you sounded perfect on the phone. I always say you can tell a lot about a person by their voice. I know you're a writer —"

I am? Oh, right. That's what I told her. "Yes, I am."

"You don't look like a writer."

He smiled. "I don't?"

"No. You're too good-looking. And you must be what? About twenty-four, twenty-five?"

"Twenty-eight," he mumbled.

"Well, anyway . . . just for today, until we see how things work out, you can stay in one of the guest cottages I rent out. Take a nap. Read . . . rest. You must rest. It's going to be a long night for you. I'll be serving dinner at seven, so you can eat before you start."

Eat! Oh my God. I think I love you.

"There are six cottages. There's no electricity, and the phones are out. We had two days of bad storms. When one thing goes out here, everything's affected. Follow me."

He gulped down his coffee and followed Mrs. King out of the parlor. She paused at the door he knew contained the dead body and saw shadow movement under the door. Somebody was walking around. The living, he told himself. Not the dead.

Outside the funeral home, the snowfall had eased up and came down in light, fluffy flakes. It was a delight to his senses as they crossed the street to the Golden Horse Cabins, pretty, charming little bungalows with window boxes filled with geraniums. It looked like something out of a Swiss mountain catalogue. Up close, the bungalows were larger than they appeared. They all clustered around a long, red-bricked rectangle of sparse grass, weeds and rose bushes.

She told him to wait by the entrance of the manager's office just inside the massive Golden Horseshoe sign overhead. The place seemed empty.

Mrs. King returned with a key, and he marveled that such a hefty woman could move so briskly. He eyed the pile of multi-colored blonde curls atop her head and wondered why she wore so much artificial hair. He tried not to stare at her gigantic ass housed in a figure-hugging, knee-length lime green winter dress. She was big and tall, and he guessed her to be in her mid-fifties.

"Here we are." She unlocked the door to the first cabin. An overhead light flickered on.

"Enjoy that while it lasts," she murmured, picking up the phone. "Nope. Still dead. Well, it's not much, but it's comfortable once you get the fire going. We charge you two dollars to use the gas fire. Coins go in this box. Come for dinner at seven, okay? See you tonight!"

She left before he could ask her about money. He was about to close the door when he heard her boots thundering up the pathway again.

"I almost forgot. I'll pay you first thing in the morning, okay?"

"Okay, thanks."

"The Jewish people don't embalm so we need to bury Mr. Herxheimer quite soon. You may have more work tomorrow night. It all depends on the family."

"Not a problem."

They smiled at each other and off she went again. He felt better after the coffee and cookies and took a look around. The place was nice enough, lots of blankets and quilts in endless linen closets. The bungalow contained three bedrooms and eight beds. It had an odd, last-holiday vibe to it, but he was pleased to see somebody's leftover milk in the fridge and two English breakfast tea bags in a cupboard.

He wished the phone worked, then brushed the thought aside. Sleep. He needed sleep. He couldn't let the spirits of the dead start walking around the little town of Fawnskin. Man . . . if only I could afford the two bucks for the gas heater . . .

Across the road on the other side of North Shore Drive, a candle flickered in a purple room filled with spiritual images and fake, purple flowers in oversize jars.

"You owe me money," the gypsy snarled.

Mel Gower licked his lips, desperation seeping into his pores. The cloying scent of copal incense made him want to gag. He was certain it was part of her monstrous attack.

"Sandy, I've done my best. I've given you hundreds," he choked on his own words, "no, thousands of dollars. I have nothing left to give you."

Tears fell from his eyes, but the dark-haired woman who'd guessed his most guilty secret leaned across the table.

"I want two thousand dollars by six o'clock Friday night. If you think God's been bad to you, wait until you see what I do to you."

Mel gasped. "But that's three days!"

It was a nightmare. A total nightmare. Sandy DiNozza had gone from being a pleasant woman who struck up a conversation with him at the Fawnskin hardware store to being a voracious hound for money . . . and more.

He stood, knowing the session was over. He was thirty-five, and he hated breathing. He hated being alive. He hated the purple walls, which felt like a sickening womb. He hated knowing his hard-earned money paid for the paint. He detested everything about the place, and now, he could smell onions. Sandy's husband always cooked heavy meals in the mornings. The smell tortured his psyche, and he fought the urge to barf.

His sessions with Sandy had been getting gradually worse. He tried putting them off, but the phone calls were incessant, and his dad couldn't stand the phone ringing all the time. Coming to see her was the only thing that appeased Sandy, who gathered her cards and blew out the white candle. He stared hard when the Three of Swords landed on the table. A man in a bathtub murdered by loved ones. Betrayal.

He sucked in a breath. How did she manage it? That card of all the cards in the deck?

The copal left an unpleasant tingle at the back of his throat, making him long for water.

All the money I have paid this woman, and she's never offered me a sip of anything.

Panic filled him again. Mel had no idea where he would

9

get the money. He'd borrowed from his savings account, his dad's social security checks and now Sandy wanted his car, but Mel couldn't give it to her.

Hell hath no fury like a psychic scorned. Mel's car key dug into his palm. He glimpsed Sandy's husband staring at him from behind a beaded curtain.

The only reason Sandy had given up her quest on the vehicle was that Mel had shown her the list of repairs it needed. She didn't care that Mel relied on it for work and for taking his dad to his various medical appointments.

The car looked better than it was. Sandy had also seen the bank statements and knew that Mel had given her everything. Still, she seethed, and her anger was terrifying.

"You have three days to come up with the money," she said again.

Mel was aware of Sandy's young son gazing at her from behind the curtain. Mel's dark eyes took in the young stare. For a moment he fancied he saw pity. Or was it disgust?

He knew he should go to the police and report the extortion. But to report what Sandy had done would mean telling them . . . everything. Shame ate at him like battery acid as he emerged from the dark, stale room, his eyes blinking as they focused on the Golden Horse Cabins across the road.

Mrs. King waved goodbye to a guy in the doorway of one of the cabins. She had a new tenant. Lucky her. Mel took a deep breath, the cool mountain air fortifying him. For a moment he could believe it was all a nightmare. He wanted to stick out his tongue and catch a snowflake, but reality blew back in his face.

I am stuck with Sandy DiNozza until one of us dies . . .

Penny Tresean absentmindedly chewed on a vanilla bean and removed it, the pungent taste flooding her senses, making her eyes water. She spat out a tiny seed from the pod.

"Pop," she growled, "I swear there's someone in there."

Her father looked up from his soupy oatmeal, a thin mix of milk and drool dripping from his protruding bottom lip. His cloudy eyes reflected no change of emotion, no semblance of surprise, or even annoyance.

She turned back to the window, inching it open a little more. In spite of the pale sun high in the sky, it was very cold. Winter had descended with a vengeance on Fawnskin. She gazed up at the blue sky, white puffy clouds floating high, her gaze returning to the log cabin perched on the north side of Big Bear Lake.

At first, she thought she imagined it because snow had started to fall. White clouds rushed across the sky, and she saw it again.

Yes! Somebody was at the window. There'd been a slight scurry of movement. Now, nothing.

Pop reacted then. "Penny, close the window."

She was so surprised he'd emerged from his befuddled mental wanderings, she closed the window again, keeping a sharp watch on the cabin across the way. She had an order for three-dozen kosher blueberry muffins and for four-dozen kosher lemon bars from the funeral parlor. It had lifted her spirits to get orders again. She had no idea what kosher muffins meant, however, and had managed to look it up online until she lost her wireless signal.

There were no animal products involved and she never cooked meat anyway, so her cooking pans qualified as kosher. She'd bought fresh blueberries that hadn't been cheap. Stirring them into her batter, she reflected on the Lenson cabin across the way. There'd been an actor who'd come up here from Big Bear itself. He'd rented the cabin while he was doing high-altitude training for some big, fancy boxing movie back in LA. He'd wanted to buy it, but Mrs. Lenson, who owned it, had died before they could come to terms.

Penny, who knew everything about everything going on in Fawnskin, knew that Mrs. Lenson's son and daughter hadn't been able to agree to anything to do with her estate and the cabin had been vacant for over a year. They couldn't even agree on a renter for the cabin. Now, all of a sudden, somebody had shown up. She'd be damned if she let some squatter move in and take over the property.

"Pop," she said, abandoning her food preparation, "I'm going over there."

She took her Akubra off the peg by the back door, slipped on gumboots, both bought via mail order catalogue, and whistled for Phoenix.

The terrier mix barreled out the back door between her legs. Penny heard her own feet crunching on the frozen grass that would be gone in a matter of days. I hand-seeded this damned thing. Pop said I was wasting my time. Damn it, he was right. Phoenix ran from one plant to the next, absorbing all the fresh new scents.

At the cabin across the road, she stopped outside the weathered wooden fence and stared at it. What should she do? If she knocked on the door, would the squatter answer it?

Should she go around the back and check things out?

She hesitated only a moment before whistling for Phoenix. "Come on, girl." They rounded the side of the house. Phoenix appeared unconcerned, but Penny paused again as they reached the back corner of the cabin. She could smell smoke. She was certain of it. She'd also been there long enough to know that Fawnskin attracted rich celebrities who enjoyed their privacy . . . and a few dangerous kooks who were a little free-wheeling with their guns.

"Come on, baby," she whispered to Phoenix. "Let's go home."

Phoenix looked disappointed. Her tail dipped just a little. Penny was always amazed at the dog's range of emotions. She relented and walked a little down the street with him. She quickly turned her head and glimpsed movement at a side window of the cabin.

Oh yes, somebody's there all right. I'll flush him out, one way or another. She wondered if she should call the Lenson heirs and warn them of the swatter. Maybe there's money in it?

CHAPTER TWO

"You're going to have to leave."

Adrian raised himself on an elbow and stared at his new lover with utter desolation.

What did I do wrong? We had an amazing time . . . I can still feel his lips on my skin . . . holy heck, the things he did to me last night.

Adrian shook the thoughts from his head and pondered his words carefully. Rallus dropped the flimsy lace curtain out from which he'd been peeking and paced the room. In daylight, Rallus was even more handsome than Adrian had thought. The room, though . . . the bedroom belonged to an old lady, not a hot, hung stud. He tried not to look like he was staring but this was definitely the work of an old lady with a fetish for lace. He stared up at the top of an ancient wardrobe. And dolls. Lots and lots of baby dolls. Their sightless eyes were a little unnerving. It was like being scrutinized by a bunch of Stepford babies.

His glance flew back to Rallus. What's the matter with him? He's so jumpy.

Rallus seemed to be undergoing several mood changes in just a few seconds. He clenched and unclenched his fists and Adrian, emboldened by his distraction, looked further around the room. Wow. They were everywhere. Some of the dolls looked real. A baby boy in a bassinet was so lifelike, it gave him a jolt.

"I know it's weird, right?"

Adrian couldn't keep his gaze off the baby boy.

"They're all over the frickin' house," Rallus griped. "Anatomically correct dolls, if you can believe it."

"Really?"

Rallus moved back to the curtain.

"Who's out there?" Adrian asked, keeping his voice soft, in spite of his fear of the creepy-looking doll.

Rallus radiated contained energy, like a caged beast, not unlike the way he'd been last night when Adrian had met him, but this was something else. Hunted. Yes, hunted. He was no longer the new guy in town anxious for cock, prowling for sexual contact.

He remembered the way Rallus had blindfolded him on the drive, and had he not been completely intoxicated by the man's presence, Adrian would have been petrified. He could have been in the hands of a serial killer.

"I don't know." Rallus glanced at him. His dark eyes gleamed at Adrian, and the man on the bed knew there was still some hunger there.

Rallus's voice came out in a sigh. "Some woman. And a dog." He ran his hand over his close-cropped, jet-black hair. "I'm a private man. I hate . . . scrutiny."

"I know you do. Come here, baby."

A muscle in Rallus's cheek twitched, and his nostrils flared, but he came to the bed, crawling across the thick covers. Naked and muscular without being over-the-top, he was a marvelous specimen.

"Mmm . . . you're hard," Adrian murmured. He had become fixated with Rallus's huge, uncut cock, never having experienced one before. He held it reverently in his fingers as Rallus hovered over him and sucked one of Adrian's nipples into his mouth. Adrian jumped. His body was so finely tuned to this stranger's touch that it responded to the smallest amount of pressure.

Rallus grunted. "Hmm. Something's going on here." He

reached down and grabbed Adrian's cock. Adrian felt inse-
cure about his dick in comparison with Rallus's majestic
weapon, but Rallus had spent a lot of time lavishing it with
his warm, ravenous mouth.

His mouth went back to it now, and Adrian's body arched
toward him. Adrian watched his lover lick the slit, and then
kiss it. Rallus sucked Adrian's cockhead into his mouth, released it, kissed the tip again, and with a sly smile, swallowed his cock whole.

Adrian almost exploded but held off as Rallus came off
his cock again.

"Put the blindfold back on," Rallus ordered, and Adrian
obeyed. He would in that moment have done anything Rallus asked of him.

Knox awoke to heavy pounding on his door. He reached for
Curtis and realized he wasn't there. Curtis was with his
folks. Man, he missed the feel of skin on fur. His heart raced
as he got out from under the pile of bedding and stumbled
to the door.

Mrs. King almost fell into the room. "What took you so
long? And why is it so cold in here?" She glanced around as
if expecting cocktail parties or some illicit poker playing.

"Sorry, I fell asleep."

"Why didn't you get the fire going?"

"I don't have any quarters."

"You should have said. Listen, we have an emergency.
My son can't sit with Mr. Herxheimer anymore. His wife
needs him. Any chance you can take over?"

"Oh, yeah, not a problem."

Knox fumbled for his coat and hoped she wouldn't notice
his worn patches.

"I'm going to sew up those holes for you," she said, sticking her finger right through one he thought he'd done a good job of hiding right by his left wrist.

They walked from his little bungalow, and he saw the afternoon sun was setting. He checked his watch. Five o'clock. He glanced at a beautiful Aspen tree by the entrance.

"That is a splendid tree," he said.

"Isn't it?" She beamed over her shoulder. "Walmart!"

He laughed. "And here's me thinking it had to be a hundred years old."

Her eyes widened. "For real. I don't know what's going on with the soil in this town, but everything grows huge."

She threw her arms wide to illustrate her point and almost got pinned by a passing truck as she stepped off the curb.

Knox pulled her off the road toward him. "Whoa!"

"You almost had two dead bodies to watch over." She cackled, and they ran across to the other side of the road.

She opened her front door, and he detected roasting potatoes.

"You can help yourself to food. I made corned beef and potatoes. You're not a vegetarian are you?"

He shook his head. He was afraid if he opened his mouth, the drool would pour from his lips.

"Did you bring anything to read? Laptop? Tsk! I didn't give you much time. Look, make up a small plate quickly and eat what you can. I'll warm the rest of it up later. You can read and work with Mr. Herxheimer, but you can't eat or drink with him. It's considered disrespectful since he can't eat or drink himself."

But he can read and use a laptop?

"Help yourself to a paperback from the library. I'll come and check on you in a couple of hours and give you a restroom break, okay?"

"Okay."

In the kitchen, he shoveled as much food as he could manage onto a dinner plate and forked it down his throat. He helped himself to a bottle of water from the fridge and gulped at it. His body reacted to the food with unbridled joy and a persistent gurgling sound. He longed for some more corned beef and a potato. He was about to spoon some onto his plate. Dismayed to find the muffins and cookies had vanished, he debated picking up an orange from the fruit bowl and turned to find Mrs. King beckoning him.

"My son is getting restless. Come and choose a book quickly."

It killed him to leave all that lovely food, but he left the plate on the countertop and followed her. She pointed to a shelf with popular paperback and hardback books in a tiny, stuffed room otherwise loaded with matching leather volumes. He picked out a Harry Potter book. He'd never read one and now was as good a time as any. He saw on the spine it was volume two and his hand fell on volume one as well. May as well stock up on everything now.

Shuffling behind Mrs. King with his books and his courage, he felt himself tensing as they arrived at the room. He hadn't expected to be shocked by the appearance of the shrouded body on the floor, or by the annoyed expression on Mrs. King's son's face.

"Finally!"

Mrs. King made hurried introductions.

"Jason, this is our new employee, Knox Baylor—"

Jason King brushed past them as Knox placed his books on the small covered table against the wall. It contained candles, matches, a reading lamp, some magazines, and a notebook and pencils in a woven basket.

Mrs. King patted his shoulder. "He's a little distracted. They're new parents, and the baby's a bit fussy. Make yourself comfortable. The air in here is deliberately chill, I'm sorry . . . you know, for obvious reasons."

She gestured at the covered body on the floor, surrounded by lit votive candles in tiny glass holders.

"Have fun. Mr. Herxheimer is quite lovely company, really, once you get to know him." She let loose a weird laugh.

"I'll see you in a little while."

She closed the door, and Knox was finally alone. Sitting with the dead.

Adrian felt the kiss going on forever. Rallus's mouth broke away from him and traveled over Adrian's chin and jawline, his hand rubbing at his cock. Adrian felt like he was still coming. The illusion was shattered as Rallus removed the blindfold and he felt the sharp rays of sunlight pricking his eyes.

"Can't I . . . can't I ever see you again?"

Rallus stared at Adrian's mouth. "Yeah, maybe."

"How do I get in touch with you?"

Rallus smiled. "You left your number on a piece of paper at my house, remember?"

"You saw that?"

Rallus chuckled.

He was so beautiful. His skin the color of coffee, dark, dark eyes Adrian was certain were black, his jet-black hair cropped short. He was around five feet ten inches, but he exuded power and strength. He exuded life.

Adrian hesitated and finally opened the door. "You were the best thing to happen in my life in a very long time."

"Yeah," Rallus said, and for a moment a shimmer of warmth welled between them. "It was great for me, too. You're a hot guy, Adrian."

He leaned over and kissed Adrian's throat, his tongue ranging over Adrian's collarbone.

"All this butter. That's what you are, butter. I can't believe nobody's snapped you up."

Adrian smiled, but his heart was breaking. Butter. *If I'm so great, how come you blindfold me and drop me in a frickin' parking lot?*

He got out of the car and walked to his own, still sitting outside the back door of Oil Can Louie's. *I bet I never see him again.* He was surprised that Rallus waited in his black pickup truck to see that Adrian's own old jalopy started okay. Then he remembered this was how they met. His car wouldn't start and Rallus, who'd been leaving the bar at the same time, offered to help.

Adrian blushed thinking about how they'd dry-humped against the pickup truck. This had been the most sensuous experience of his life.

This time, his car engine turned over easily. When he turned to wave goodbye, the black pickup truck was already rolling back onto the highway, back into Fawnskin.

As he came out of the parking lot, Adrian spotted a guy in a vintage Mustang driving into it.

Adrian recognized him as the bartender from the night before, Mel. They exchanged a friendly wave. Mel would be here to set up happy hour, but Mel didn't seem too happy.

That's a guy with a lot on his mind.

Adrian's thoughts returned to Rallus.

Butter. Holy heck that guy was amazing. I wonder if he's living in Fawnskin . . . maybe I could track him down?

"Come in and have a beer," Mel called out.

Adrian thought about it. Maybe Rallus would come in. Maybe he just needed to wait.

Rallus walked into the Fawnskin General Store, tickled at the goods on display. He felt like he'd stepped back in time being in this town. Time. He brushed the thought away. He was ecstatic that Fawnskin had no big chain stores. It needed a bookstore, though. It, along with several other shops appeared to have recently gone under, but not the General Store. It smelled good. Sex always made him hungry, and he felt encouraged by the warm, chatty atmosphere.

Foodstuffs made up a good portion of the products on display. There was also a hot food bar with fried chicken, massive sandwiches, and two kinds of pizza. His gaze strayed to a frozen food section featuring three kinds of gelato and a dozen different ice creams.

He tried samples and bought a ton of stuff. The gleaming fishing rods made him wish he was interested in that hobby. There were picnic chairs, umbrellas, camping goods. A well-stocked organic food section featured freshly baked goods and local fruits and vegetables.

Rallus debated on fresh flowers when he overheard a snippet of conversation.

"I can help you," a woman said.

"I don't want your help," a second woman said, her voice low. She sounded fearful and anxious, but the first woman's syrupy tones belied a very pushy nature.

"Oh, but you do need my help. You think your life is bad now? It's only going to get worse, Penny."

"Who . . . who are you? Why won't you leave me alone?"

Rallus looked up between shelves of canned goods and his eyes locked with a woman opposite him. She had streaked blonde hair. She blinked in surprise and glanced back at the other woman, a brunette, whom he could only partially see. Her hands covered her face.

The pushy blonde must have seen something in his eyes that made her change her mind, and she walked quickly out of the store. The brunette dropped her hands, her tear-stained face registering shock as she stared after the departing woman.

Rallus realized it was the woman who'd been outside his house.

He stepped away quietly so she wouldn't realize he was watching her. He paid for his food and, outside, a small terrier waited. He recognized it as the woman's dog. He looked up and down the street for the first woman and spied her entering a building farther up the hill. He walked up to it, but she was long gone. Outside her pink and purple store were pink geraniums in a window box and a purple lamp shone from behind a lavender curtain. A small sign in the window read, by appointment only.

She's either a whore or a gypsy fortune teller. I'm betting a bit of both.

Rallus listened for movement, heard nothing and walked away, but knew the gypsy whore was watching him. He gave her a finger wave over his shoulder and smiled to himself.

Sandy stepped back from the window. *Damn. Who was this guy?* She'd almost put the bite on Penny. Something about him frightened her. No. *She feared no man. He angered her. He's taking the food out of my family's mouths. I will fix him.*

She turned and found her husband, Steve, watching her.

"Well?"

She shrugged.

He sighed. "Maybe we should fish in a bigger pool. We've only got three clients, and they're almost spent. I'm worried that Mel Gower will go to the cops. We can't afford to screw him too tight to the wall."

"No, he's not going to do that." Sandy knew Mel Gower's type. He was gay and stupid and gullible. He was not smart enough to fight her. He'd surprised her by not giving up the car. Maybe he wasn't as weak as he seemed.

"Maybe we should take a drive up to Arrowhead on Saturday and hit the street market," Steve said.

"Sure." But her heart wasn't in it. She wanted the Mustang, and she wanted Penny Tresean to realize her mistake. Penny needed to pay. Penny needed to pay big.

"Maybe we should think about moving . . . you know up to Big Bear."

"Not yet," she said. "I think that guy has money. I want one more big client. Then we leave."

"Who is he?"

"No idea. But I'll find out."

Mel Gower wiped down the bar again. Six guys here for happy hour. Sandy did this. As soon as she started her lotions and potions, my business ran to shit. Look at this! Nobody's here!

He stared at the guy down the end who kept glancing at the front door every time the wind blew it open.

Mel went over and gestured to the customer's empty Bombay and tonic. "Like another?"

The guy blinked and focused on him as if realizing for the first time where he was.

"No . . . I don't know. I don't know what I want."

The guy looked lost, and Mel hoped he wasn't a headcase. The mountains were full of weird guys who turned up out of nowhere. Sometimes they'd blown all their money in Vegas and, too afraid to face their wives back in LA, they detoured up here. They'd hole up a day or two and head home. Sometimes they stayed.

Fawnskin used to be an artists' colony, and a major stagecoach stop back in the day. It still attracted an interesting crowd. Though it still had its fair share of arty type folks, there were guys hiding out in cabins who'd done long prison stretches and preferred to keep their peace with a gun stretched across their knees.

Mel was pretty good at reading guys and knew this newcomer was none of these. This guy had gambled all right, but probably on love.

"How about some coffee?" he asked. "On the house."

The customer blinked again and then smiled.

"I'd like that. Thanks."

Knox grew uncomfortable sitting in the chair reading. The room was silent, and he could no longer detect the smell of gas he'd noticed when he first entered. He knew dead bodies released gases, but he convinced himself it had been Jason, the previous shomerim who'd been farting, not poor Mr. Herxheimer lying on the floor.

The old man's outline haunted him. It's really a body under that sheet.

He kept staring for signs of movement. An hour and forty-five minutes he'd been here, and he was restless. In fifteen minutes, Mrs. King would relieve him. He'd have to eat fast, and he thought about the long night ahead of him.

I know I can do this, yes I can.

He listened for any movement in the house. Nothing. He was alone. He cracked open the Harry Potter book, The Sorcerer's Stone again. The first chapter, which depicted gross child abuse had upset him. He'd experienced enough in his own life. He felt guilty about leaving Curtis with his folks.

No, they love dogs. They just don't love children.

He turned his attention back to the character Albus Dumbledore, talking to a tabby cat, who was really a woman. He wondered if Mr. Herxheimer would enjoy having

Knox read to him aloud.

My parents never read aloud to me. I would have liked that. He turned a page. Dammit, I can smell that food. I'm so hungry.

Feeling foolish about reading aloud to a dead body, he resumed his literary adventures in silence.

Adrian twirled the coffee cup in his hand. Mel gave him a refill, feeling guilty. He was supposed to be the one making his patrons feel better, not the other way around. It was just him and Adrian alone in the bar now.

"This is good coffee," Adrian said. "Your menu looks great. I'm sorry you're having such a tough time of things."

"Thanks." You don't know the half of it.

"You know, your bar isn't . . . no offense meant, but it's not grungy enough to attract the hard-core drunks and not quite . . . classy enough to make people want to come in and try out the food."

He glanced around the room. "I mean, look at this wall over there. The paneling is superb, and I love the color. That sage green is very happening. Very now. You've done part of the other wall, too, but you stopped at the fireplace. That's a great feature by the way. You should make more use of it. Is it functional?"

"Yeah," Mel mumbled, feeling his blood pressure rising. Everything Adrian said was true. He'd had great visions for this place. He's imagined a big leather sofa, a couple of big easy chairs to match, ottomans. He'd even picked out the furniture he wanted in a catalogue.

And then I met Sandy. Man, she is killing me. I've given her everything, and she still wants more. He glanced out the window to make sure his car was still there. He was worried the gypsy would steal it. She really had a hard-on for his old

Mustang.

"I'm so sorry," he said.

"Don't worry on my account. You know, you need a big leather sofa . . . right over there. Maybe a couple of big chairs—"

"That's exactly how I see it!" Mel was ecstatic. "And then I was thinking ottomans . . . maybe an Asian daybed—"

"Wow. That sounds cool."

Mel stared at him. "Are you an interior designer? I mean, you seem to know a lot about this sort of thing."

Adrian smiled. "Oh, yeah. Actually, I'm an architect. I wear my passion on my sleeve."

"You're new around here, right?"

"I'm not really from around here. I moved to Big Bear last month. I came to look at a place I'm supposed to be working on a . . ." He took a deep breath. "You know Rallus?"

Mel frowned. "Rallus? No, don't think I do."

"I met him here last night."

"No . . . I don't think I know him. He lives here in Fawn-skin?"

"I don't know to be honest. I had incredible sex with him."

Mel stared at him. "Wow. And you met him here?"

Adrian laughed. "Yep." He leaned across the bar. "He blindfolded me, drove me home and sent me to paradise."

"He blindfolded you?"

"Yep."

Mel shuddered. "Shit. He sounds freaky."

Adrian stared into his cup. "I can't believe I'm telling you this." He looked up again, blushing. "I can't believe I did it."

"I can't believe you did it either, but I'm glad you're okay."

"Thanks. Me, too."

Mel felt a sharp pang of jealousy. He felt something . . . a stirring of feelings for Adrian. Feelings he never thought he would find again. *Ah, what's the use? He's got the hots for some weirdo with a blindfold.*

The door opened, and Penny walked in.

"Hey, sis, how ya doin'? How's Pop?" He leaned over the counter and kissed her cold cheek.

"I'm fine." She smiled at Adrian. "Hi."

"Hi."

Mel introduced them. "Penny, this is Adrian . . ."

"Harris," Adrian said, shaking her hand.

She unwound a long woolen scarf from her neck. "I can't stay. Just wanted to make sure you know Pop needs to go to the doctor at seven in the morning."

"Don't worry. I'll get up in time."

"I couldn't call. Phones are still down."

"Oh, tell me about it. You'll be okay getting home on your own?"

"I'm fine," she said again and gave him a wave. She wrapped her scarf around her neck again and left.

Mel felt the tears and tension hovering in a persistent haze over his spirit.

"She's a cutie pie," Adrian said.

"Yeah. Her husband was killed by a drunk driver last year. Killed him and their two kids. She moved up here with me and Pop. Don't think we're much company for her."

"Oh. Man, that sucks. I'm sorry."

Mel nodded. "Thanks."

"Hey, I think I'll splurge and get the fish and chips."

The lights faltered, and the place fell into darkness.

"Maybe not," Adrian said, and the lights came back on again.

"Generator," Mel said, with a confident grin. "It's hard to destroy us mountaineers."

"I'll drink to that." Adrian held out his cup and Mel refilled it. Rallus. He's a freak. I'm not.

"Thanks, Mel. And thanks for not making me feel any more stupid than I do about Rallus. The more I think about it, the more I feel like crap for letting him blindfold me. I'm betting you'd never do that to a guy."

Mel grinned. "Only if he asked me to."

Their shared laughter released some tension. Mel felt his spirits lift just a little.

"It's been a long time for me," Adrian said. "I let my hair down." He leaned back on his stool. "You're a great guy, Mel. Thanks for listening to me."

Mel grinned and moved toward the open-plan kitchen in back of the bar to cook. His heart sang as he heated the griddle, his gaze on the man at the bar who smiled back at him.

Maybe . . . maybe I have a chance with a guy like this. This is a real sweet guy.

Knox needed to pee. He needed to go so bad his head ached. Three hours he'd been here and Mrs. King hadn't relieved him. *Relief . . . oh God. Why did I have to think that word? Now I'm gonna pee my pants.* He got up and kept his eyes on the body.

"Forgive me," he whispered and ran from the room. He barely made it to the bathroom before he unzipped his pants. Terror almost froze him. He'd left Mr. Herxheimer alone. He was afraid to flush the toilet and give away his secret if somebody entered the house and heard the noise. He was also afraid not to flush it and be disgusting. He flushed it and ran, scuttling back to the room.

The body on the floor was gone.

Penny let herself into the house and checked the oven. Oh,

thank God. She'd made it back in time. She grabbed the last two pans out using her mitts and gave the pans a critical look. Perfect.

"Where's dinner?" her father asked from the next room.

"Coming right up, Pop."

"I'm hungry. I want a yogurt."

He whizzed into the kitchen in his brand-new wheelchair, and she made a grab for the fridge. Dad had a way of dropping everything. Too late. He dropped the carton of yogurt, and it splattered to the floor.

She knelt and cleaned up the mess. Pop started to moan.

"What's happening to me?" he asked. "What's going on, Pen?"

"Oh, Pop." She held his thin, bony body against hers and fought the urge to cry.

She reached across to her Envirosac and took out a fresh carton of yogurt. He was fussing and whining like a child. She pulled back the foil-top opening and gave him a spoon.

"Wheel me in?" he asked, and she pushed his wheelchair into the living room. She made sure he ate a couple of bites before he forgot what he was doing, before he forgot to eat. She gave him the TV remote, and he wielded it like a weapon. Pow! Entertainment Tonight. Zap! BBC World News. Thunk! An outraged Nancy Grace. Pop stared, fixated as the helmet-haired Grace howled, "Tonight, where is little Hayleigh? Where is this beautiful little two-year-old girl?"

"I need to take the muffins and cakes to the funeral home. I won't be long."

But Pop was lost in the latest missing child case. Hard to believe he was once one of Fawnskin's finest . . .

Rallus considered going back to the bar. He thought about it for a good hour before deciding he had to have a drink, had to be around people . . . Yeah, why the hell not? It was too damned quiet and he knew nothing else would be open.

His thoughts drifted to Adrian. He was sorry now he'd thrown out the guy's number, but maybe it was for the best. He got into his truck and rolled down the street . . . sure was quiet in this neck of the woods.

Knox closed the door on the room with the corpse. Or, the missing corpse. How could it be missing? He must be imagining things. His heart pounded in his chest. Everybody could hear it, he was certain. Who?

You screwed up again, maestro. Try explaining a missing corpse. Where the hell was everyone? One bleak light was on in the hallway and he heard strange sounds. Oh fuck. Mr. Herxheimer's ghost is wandering. He freaked out, convinced he could pick out shadows in the darkness. Oh my God, he's a dybbuk. It's happened. It's really happened!

When he leaned against the closed door and rested his head back, a shadow crossed his eyes. He jumped. Outside the front door, he heard somebody jiggling the handle. Locked. Oh, God. He heard knocking and then the person rang the bell. A key. Somebody had a key and was coming in.

He couldn't be out here. He frantically opened the door to the room and closed it behind him. He swallowed and felt the fear stuck in his throat. The room felt colder than ever. He couldn't bear to turn around and see the empty space. A cold wet sensation crept across his right heel. Knox gasped.

Please, oh please . . . make this be a nightmare . . .

Sandy took the garbage outside. Steve was useless with some things, like earning money, paying bills and remembering things like anniversaries and birthdays. No, his gifts lay in other areas like using spy equipment to eavesdrop on neighbors and use the information against them.

Snow was on the air again. She opened the trash can lid and caught movement out of the corner of her eye. She started, until she saw who it was.

"What are you doing here?" she asked.

"Surprised?" he asked.

"Um . . . er . . ." Where the hell is Steve? "A little. Nice to see you again."

"Really." He let out a harsh laugh. "You don't look like it's nice to see me again. You look a little . . ."

"Tired," she said quickly.

"Frightened," he responded.

"Are you frightened of me?" he asked, stepping closer to her.

"No. Should I be?"

Her knees started to shake above her new Ugg boots. Man, he was acting weird.

"Well, you should be," he said. "You really should be."

She opened her mouth, and he slugged her. She hit the ground hard, her head bouncing off the slushy snow.

Sandy lay on the ground stunned that'd he actually laid a hand on her.

"Don't," she said.

"Don't what?"

"Don't kill me."

"I'm not going to kill you, you money whore. We're going to play a little game. Okay?"

She screamed as he put his full body force into a kick to her head.

Knox stood petrified as the door opened and Mrs. King

poked her head around the corner.

"I'm so sorry. I went to the hairdresser's and lost track of time. She's my daughter, so we tend to chat. How's Mr. Herxheimer doing?"

"Fine," he said. *Oh my God, oh my God. How do I explain? Can I go to jail for this?*

She beamed at him. "I'll sit with him a few minutes while you take a potty break and grab something to eat. I'm afraid you're going to be on your own all night, so eat as much as you can."

Mrs. King brushed past him, and Knox's heart leapt to his throat.

"But—"

He was stunned when he realized the body was back on the floor.

How the . . .

"Quickly now," she said, shooing him away like a crazy fly.

Hunger replaced anguish. *I imagined it. Yes, I imagined the whole thing.*

He left the room, and he felt the skittering feeling of ice cold fingers brushing across his face. He almost screamed when the front doorbell rang.

"Get that, will you?" Mrs. King poked her head out again.

Now that he looked at her, Knox, who'd been raised by a woman addicted to weekly visits with the hairdresser, realized Mrs. King had been lying. Her hair looked no different than when he'd last seen her. *Why is she lying? Where has she been?*

"Not a problem," he said aloud and opened the front door.

"Hi," said a woman standing on the stoop, a plastic container in her hands.

"Is that Penny?" Mrs. King yelled down the hallway.

Penny Tresean laughed. "It's me." She held out a hand to Knox, who shook it, and they introduced themselves.

She stepped inside the front door and cast a furtive look around.

"Here are the rest of the cakes for tomorrow's Lev . . . Lev . . ." She pulled a piece of paper from her pocket. "Levayah. Have I said it right?"

"I . . . er . . . yes," he said, not wanting to make her feel bad even though he had no clue.

"Knox, bring me my checkbook," Mrs. King shouted from the corpse-watching room. "It's in the kitchen."

Knox and Penny deposited the cakes on the countertop, and he hunted around for Mrs. King's checkbook.

"It's in the breadbox," Mrs. King shouted and he lifted the lid and indeed found it in there.

"Can you wait here a moment?" he asked Penny.

"Sure."

He returned to the corpse-watching room. Mrs. King looked pale.

"This is so creepy being here at night. Isn't this creepy to you?"

"No," he said. "I find it peaceful."

A frigid finger raked across the back of his neck, and he felt terror ignite his very soul.

"What's Levayah?" he asked her.

She stared at him in confusion. "Oh. It means accompaniment. Mr. Herxheimer is to be buried the day after tomorrow. We're waiting for some of his relatives to arrive from New York. A few will be here tomorrow to visit with him, a kind of a knees-up . . . You know, a somber one before we sit . . . you know, vigil again tomorrow night."

Mrs. King scribbled out a check and tore it out of the book.

"Give this to Penny. Can you eat quickly?" she asked.

"I'm feeling real funny being alone here with the corpse."

"Not a problem."

He returned to the kitchen and gave Penny her check.

"Thanks so much," she said, looking relieved. "You're new here, aren't you?"

"I am." God, I'm starving. Oh, no . . . there's hardly any food left. Where did it all go? There's been nobody here!

He scooped what was left in the pan onto a clean plate and hefted spoonfuls into his mouth.

"Sorry," he said. "I'm ravenous, and I'm corpse-watching until ten o'clock tomorrow morning."

"Wow," she said. "This funeral's really huge. I know there's all kinds of rules for the flowers, the mourners" — she gestured at her food containers — "the food, everything."

He nodded. His meal was over in a few sad bites, and he reached for an orange.

Mrs. King yelled for him.

"Coming," he said, as he tore into the orange.

Penny took the fruit from his clumsy fingers. "Here, let me."

"You have kids?"

She shook her head. "A dad with dementia."

"I'm so sorry."

"Me, too." She let out a sigh as she handed perfectly peeled segments to Knox. "He has good days and bad days."

"Knox!"

"I gotta go," he said, mumbling around a mouthful of food.

Penny smiled. "A man's gotta do what a man's gotta do."

Sandy woke with a start. She was on the sofa, her husband Steve beside her, watching The First 48 on TV. He stared at the TV, and she almost cried with relief. It was a nightmare.

Geez, but her head hurt.

"Wow, I had the freakiest dream."

"You did?"

He yawned and stretched.

"Yeah." She felt irritable now. "Why do you watch this show? It's so . . . disturbing."

"Because I learn things from it, Sandra. And in our line of work, we can't have too much knowledge or be too careful."

"But Michael—"

"Michael's asleep."

He switched off the TV and dumped the remote on the coffee table.

"I have a bad feeling."

Steve laughed, but it wasn't a happy sound. "Oh please, babe. You don't have a psychic bone in your body."

"Don't say that."

He shrugged. "It's true." He got up and stalked off to the bedroom.

She felt terrible. Her head pounded as if she really had been kicked and she thought again about the dream. No, a horrible, horrible nightmare.

Steve and I fight all the time now. We're making money. Why are things so bad between us?

She fought off sleepiness long enough to brush her teeth and check on Michael. He was asleep. She stepped into the room but changed her mind about tucking him in. A light sleeper, her six-year-old would likely wake up and demand milk and more bedtime stories. She closed the door again and walked down the hallway to her bedroom. Steve was already asleep. As usual.

Sandy was surprised to see a lit candle sitting on the bureau. How dangerous. Why had he left a lit candle there unattended? She shook him awake. Screw his sleep. With the winds whistling through the old house's windows, he should never have left the candle there. Steve stirred, and when his eyes opened, she realized he'd fallen quickly into a deep sleep.

"Why did you leave the candle there?" she asked.

"I didn't."

"Come on," she said. "I'm tired, and I don't feel good."

"I'm telling you, I didn't put it there."

They stared at each other a moment and a strange creaking sound, followed by a sudden thud, interrupted their silent war.

"Michael," Sandra said and ran to his room.

His door was open when she reached it. With a shaky hand, she flipped on the light. Michael was gone.

CHAPTER THREE

He fought the urge, like the devil, to sleep. For the last two hours, the need had been strong. Knox wanted so badly to sleep that he battled it by moving about the room. He walked and talked to himself, read the book aloud to Mr. Herxheimer, whom he was sure was getting a kick out of Harry Potter, boy wizard.

"I feel deprived that I never got to go to a school like Hogwarts," he suddenly said to Mr. Herxheimer. "How about you? What was school like for you? How old were you when you lost your virginity?"

He felt that weird cold finger of ice on the back of his neck and jumped.

Knox opened the door. The world was in darkness when he glimpsed the sky from the front windows way down the end of the hall.

He sighed and came back into the room. He needed to pee. He needed to sleep.

"Hello?" he said aloud down the hallway.

He knew nobody was here, but he couldn't resist shouting it. The urge to pee grew so strong he had to go, and he darted to the small powder room, keeping up a conversation with Mr. Herxheimer as he hosed the toilet bowl.

"Harold," said a voice loud and clear.

Knox almost screamed. He turned, zipping up his fly and could swear he heard a rustle of movement, saw a turn of an ankle at the door. He groped for the toilet flush and made it across to the room with the dead body.

Still there.

He heard voices at the front door and stood still as Mrs. King's booming motherly voice called out . . .

"Knox!"

He poked out his head.

She beamed at him. "Need to pee?"

"Er, yes," he said, and as soon as she was at his door, he scuttled across the room.

"Brrrrr . . ." she said. "It's freezing in here."

He ran back to the bathroom and washed his face and hands. He felt immediately better.

"Can you sit with Mr. Herxheimer again tonight?" she asked.

"Harold," said the strange voice again.

Knox blinked. "Did you hear that?"

"Hear what?"

I'm hearing things.

"I can hear the wind . . . anyway. Sure. I can work tonight." Oh, God . . . I don't know if I can handle another night like this one. But crap. I need the money. "Sure. I can do it."

Mrs. King looked relieved. "I'm gonna make coffee. You want some toast?"

He nodded eagerly. He checked his watch as soon as she left the room. It was seven o'clock. A few more hours. Man, but it was dark outside.

A male voice laughed, and he wanted to run from the room. Instead, he sat in silence, looking at the blank walls, and felt grateful for another human in the house.

When she came in to tell him there was food in the kitchen, he asked, "What is Mr. Herxheimer's first name?"

"Harold," she said, and he wasn't surprised, but the laughter tickling his ear was anything but funny.

He scuttled to the kitchen where he ate two pieces of toast

and downed half a cup of coffee when the doorbell rang.

"Can you get that?" Mrs. King called.

His hand was on the door when she came running.

"Go back to the room. I'll get it. I'll relieve you as soon as I can."

She waited until he was back in the room and he heard her opening the door.

"Hi," said the ghostly voice and he heard that laughter again, making him shake right there in his shoes.

A few seconds later he heard a light tap at the door, and he stepped back as Mrs. King entered. She was accompanied by a young woman he recognized as being the girl in overalls on the cookie. Her clothes were torn on one side, and so were the clothes on the young man standing by her.

"The family wishes to visit Mr. Herxheimer," Mrs. King said, inclining her head meaningfully toward the kitchen.

"Of course," Knox said and slipped from the room.

The couple closed the door, and once they were in the kitchen, Knox asked Mrs. King about the torn clothes.

"It is part of their religious custom."

The front doorbell rang, and he opened it to more family members.

He was beyond tired. He was exhausted to the bone, but much preferred serving coffee, small sandwiches, and cakes to hanging out with . . . Harold.

There was a solid knock on the front door at one point, and the man standing there smiled at him. Knox almost came in his pants.

Wow, he is so freakin' hot.

"Hi, good morning," the man said.

"I'm Knox." He shook the man's hand.

"Rallus. My name is Rallus."

"You're part of the family?"

"No . . . oh . . . I saw activity. I came because —"

"Please, come in," Knox said, remembering his manners. He hoped he wasn't drooling. This guy was sex on legs.

"Knox?" Mrs. King came to the door.

"Well, you're a specimen. I mean, are you part of the family?"

Rallus smiled. "No, I'm not. I—"

He was interrupted by the blaring of a loud car horn.

It went on and on. It was disturbing in the early, still slumbering silence.

"Somebody's acting a fool," Mrs. King said.

Rallus's expression darkened. "No, they're not. That's Morse code. I grew up in St. Innocent, Alaska. I had a radio fanatic for a stepdaddy who insisted I learn Morse code. I recognize this. I've never had occasion to use it, but this is an SOS. Somebody's in trouble."

The gorgeous man ran back outside in a flash. Knox looked around for his coat. Mrs. King stepped forward and shoved it into his hands.

"I mended the holes."

"Thanks," Knox said as he shrugged into the coat. He wished he had a hat, but prayed his shaggy brown hair would cover his ears enough to escape frostbite.

When Knox got back outside, his eyes searched the horizon for Rallus. That was a man who seemed to have it all together, the kind of guy you'd want to have around in a crisis. And from the way some lady was screeching, it sure seemed like a crisis was just what they had going on.

A small crowd of people had gathered, peering curiously at the scene. As Knox moved closer, he finally got a look at the woman doing the screeching. She was in her housecoat, hair in disarray. She might have been pretty once, but even though she couldn't have been more than thirty, she looked used by life. She was pounding on Rallus's chest, and he stood there like a solid slab of concrete, not in the least bothered by it. After a few seconds, he seized her wrists, and her fit ended, just like that.

"Now, calmly tell me, where was the last place you saw him?"

"In his bed, of course," she muttered, lowering her head to rub her nose across the sleeve of the housecoat. "He'll freeze out here if you don't find him," she hollered into his face.

"I'm aware of that." He released her and stood back. "Now, go back inside." He turned and scanned the crowd. "All of you. There's nothing more to see here unless you're prepared to join the search."

"Let me just go back in and ask Mrs. King if she needs me," Knox interjected. "I'd like to help. Where in hell are the police?"

"There are two in the area. It will take them a while to get out here. Someone's already called them," Rallus replied. He seemed distracted by the task of sending people off in various directions.

Mrs. King's lined face looked concerned when Knox made it back inside. "What's going on out there? What in the devil was all that screaming about?"

"A little boy is missing. If I'm not needed, I'd like to help in the search."

"You go ahead," she muttered. "The family is here now with him."

"Thanks," Knox said and raced back outside. He spotted Rallus walking toward a big red pickup. He called out to him, causing him to pause. "Can I come with you or . . ."

"Sure," he muttered, "hop in."

Knox remained silent while Rallus started the engine. He looked preoccupied. "It's cold out here but not as cold tonight as last night so —"

"Cold enough for that kid to freeze in no time flat."

His attempt at trying to be optimistic was completely dashed by Rallus. "How would that little boy get out anyway? Do you think some weirdo kidnapped him?"

"Up here in this place?" He shifted the truck into gear and spun out of the yard. "It's most likely called a case of not watching your kid."

"Neglect." Knox tasted the word in his mouth. It was hard to say which was worse, being totally ignored or getting the shit beat out of you. It was always a toss-up.

Rallus glanced at him. "Did you say something?"

He shook his head. "So, ah . . . you're from Alaska right?"

"Among other places."

"What brought you here to this place?"

"It's as good a place to spend time as any."

Knox considered that to be an odd answer.

"I might ask you the same." Rallus scanned the road from side to side as he drove slowly through town.

"I like watching the dead. They don't give you any trouble."

He nodded. "I suppose they don't. And this is now your chosen profession, Knox?"

"Better than what I used to do."

"Which was?" He looked right at him.

Knox opened his mouth, prepared to say anything but the truth, but then Rallus said, "Look, over there. There's something moving at the side of the road down near the cemetery gates." Rallus sped up. He pulled the vehicle to the side of the road and jumped out.

Knox forced open the heavy door and followed at his heels.

"Michael?" Rallus called out, but the small figure, which was definitely that of a boy around the age of six, just kept walking as if he hadn't heard.

Rallus easily cleared the distance between them. He

clamped a hand on his shoulder and turned him around. The headlights from the pickup made his eyes look strange, as if he wasn't even there somehow. Rallus spoke to him gently, in a gentle tone. "Where are you going, Michael? Your mother is worried."

The little boy looked directly at Knox suddenly. "Where'd you find this one, Knox? He's a heartbreaker."

Knox narrowed his eyes. "Who are you?"

Rallus looked at Knox now as if he'd lost his mind. "He's that kid we're looking for of course. Who else would he be?"

Knox barely heard him. He couldn't take his eyes off the boy. "Harold?"

"Who?" Rallus demanded, losing patience, that gentle tone in his voice lost suddenly. "Come on," he muttered. He reached down and hoisted the boy up on his shoulder. "Let's get you home."

Knox walked behind Rallus as they made their way back to the truck. That kid, or whoever in hell he was, hadn't stopped staring at him. Damn it, I should have never gone to take a pee.

But I'm grateful you did. It gave me the opportunity I needed. You should really jump this guy's bones. He's hot as hell . . . isn't that the way they say it nowadays, kiddo?

"Are you talking to me?" Knox demanded. That was no six-year-old talking.

Rallus looked back at him. "I didn't say a thing."

"Not you, him, Harold."

"Why in hell are you calling him Harold?" Rallus opened the door to his truck and placed the boy inside.

Knox shook his head. He was losing it.

The child sat in the middle between them, silently watching the road as Rallus drove. He said nothing until Rallus pulled the truck up outside the house where he lived, then he looked right at Knox and said, "This should be pleasant.

She's not the boy's mother, you know?"

Rallus didn't hear that. He was out of the truck and coming round to open the door on the passenger side. "Get the boy and let's get him inside. I don't understand how come he's not blue, walking around in nothing but those flimsy pajamas.

Rallus paused as he lifted his hand to pound on the front door. There was some serious fighting going on inside. Poor kid. No wonder he ran away. When the yelling grew louder, he discarded his manners and put his shoulder to the wood. The door was unlocked and opened easily. The man and woman looked up in surprise to see him standing there.

"My hero," the boy said aloud, laughing.

Rallus stared at him, his face registering surprise at the voice which came out of him.

The woman burst into tears suddenly as she spotted her son. She raced over and took him from Knox's arms. "Oh, thank God, thank God." She hugged him to her, rocking him back and forth in her arms. "Where in the hell were you?"

"Wouldn't you like to know?" came the reply.

She narrowed her eyes. Her mouth, already looking puffy from where someone had given her a good punch, grew hard. "Don't you speak to me like that. You been picking up bad habits from these men here?"

Rallus laughed out loud. "Isn't this just dandy? I save her kid, and she accuses me of teaching him to talk nasty."

"I didn't pick up anything." Michael winked at Rallus. "Handsome bugger, isn't he? Makes Steve here look like a piece of . . ."

"I'll wash out your mouth," she threatened, putting him down. "Go to bed now!"

"So much for the reunion." He smirked and raised a hand at Knox and Rallus. "See you. And enjoy life, it's pretty damn short. You know what I'm talking about, don't you,

Rallus?"

Rallus swallowed hard.

Knox was out the door already. Shit. All this stuff was true. If you didn't watch these dead people, they got up and walked around. Hell, they invaded people's bodies. He felt sick. He heard Rallus say something about the need to watch your children more carefully, then he tossed it right there on the snow.

"Hey," Rallus said, placing a hand on his shoulder. "You okay?"

"No."

"Come on, I'll get you back home. What did you think of those people?" Rallus asked casually as he drove back in the direction of Mrs. King's.

"Strange. I think that man would've beaten the crap out of her if we hadn't arrived when we did."

"Um. They deserve each other."

"You don't like them."

"I don't trust them. I don't think she'd win any mother of the year awards."

"Think she's an abuser?"

"I don't know. I didn't see any marks on his body, at least any place that would have been noticeable. Anyway, if that's the case, I won't be letting her get away with it."

The snow was falling now. It reminded Knox of times he'd spent out in the cold all night. He would have liked to have had someone like Rallus to turn to.

Knox turned his head and rested it against the passenger window. Big, strong, brave, and sexy as hell. Rallus was a man in control of his emotions, a man who could handle any crisis.

Knox couldn't believe what Michael, Harold . . . whoever he'd been at that moment, had said, but damn it, jumping Rallus's bones sure had its appeal.

Without fully thinking through his actions, he blindly reached across the seat and put his hand on Rallus's thigh. The muscles under his palm contracted, but at least Rallus hadn't slugged him.

Even if he was pushed out of the truck with a black eye, Knox knew it was worth it. He ran his hand a little farther up Rallus's thigh and squeezed. "I imagine Michael would be grateful if you'd watch over him."

The pickup slowed to a stop. "What the hell are you doing?"

Knox wiped the errant tears from his cheeks and turned to face Rallus. How could he explain his emotions at the moment? He was freaked out by the man/boy they'd just rescued, he was feeling warm and fuzzy about Rallus's proclamation to protect Michael, and he was suddenly feeling extremely horny, a sensation he hadn't experienced in a long time. There was something about selling your ass for a couple of bucks that tended to take the fun out of sex, and something about this man that brought it all back.

"I don't know," Knox finally answered. He laughed a little uncomfortably.

Rallus reached down and repositioned Knox's hand to rest against the bulge behind his fly. "That what you want?"

Knox swallowed around the lump in his throat. Oh yeah. His hand involuntarily contracted around Rallus's filling cock. "If I say yes, are you going to beat the shit out of me?"

Rallus ground his cock against Knox's hand. "If you say yes, I'll fuck your brains out."

Knox bit his bottom lip. Despite his bark, Rallus seemed like a nice guy, maybe too nice for the likes of him. How long had it been since he'd gone to bed with a man out of want instead of financial need?

"Yes," he finally squeaked.

CHAPTER FOUR

"This feels weird."

"It's not weird."

Knox shook his head as if it might loosen some change in his piggy bank.

Rallus smiled. "Come on, it's kinda cool, don't you think?"

"No," Knox said. "I thought when the words fuck and my brains came together . . . you and I would, too. I didn't think you'd bring me here."

Rallus spread his hands. "What could I do? Your boss came out."

Knox sighed.

"I wanted to do this." Rallus's voice softened. "I wanted to be alone with you."

Knox blushed. "Yeah, well, we're alone. You, me and . . . Mr. Herxheimer."

Rallus stared at the body on the floor, covered in a linen sheet and surrounded by lit candles in votive jars. He paused to take in the faint scent of honeysuckle from the melting wax.

"Well, I wanted to see what you do. I never dated a corpse watcher before."

Knox dropped his voice. "We're not supposed to talk."

Rallus dropped his voice, too. "So, when I fuck you, you'd better be quiet. Don't want to wake the dead, do you?"

Knox looked taken aback. "You're not going to fuck me here."

"Oh, yes I am."

"Oh no—"

Footsteps in the hallway stopped their conversation. Rallus winked at Knox. Mrs. King's heavy breathing could be heard, like a wheezy wind right outside the door. She tiptoed away, and Rallus grinned.

"As I was saying . . ." He leaned across his director's chair and kissed Knox hard on the mouth. The kiss startled Knox, who resisted at first.

"Kiss me," Rallus murmured against his mouth.

"I—"

Rallus took advantage of Knox's open mouth to kiss him deeper. Knox moaned and seemed to catch his breath. Rallus pulled away, and the two men looked at each other. Rallus was enthralled by the intensity boiling between them. He could see Knox was intimidated by it.

"This is wrong," Knox said.

"It's hot," Rallus retorted. "You're absolutely fucking beautiful. Did you know that?"

Knox fumbled for a response. "Um . . . thanks." In the next breath, he said, "It's wrong."

"Why? I bet the old guy got no action in . . . probably years. I bet this is a send-off he never anticipated."

"You're probably right there."

Rallus reached for Knox. "So come here and kiss me."

Knox shook his head again, but his lips soon met Rallus's and once again the heat between them was almost unbearable. Knox leaned into Rallus's strong body, and one of the candles on the floor blew out. Both men stopped and stared at it.

"I'll light another one." Knox seemed rattled and rummaged through a basket on the table for a fresh candle. Rallus watched him. Knox was sensational. He had a touch of insecurity that was somehow refreshing. It wasn't neurosis . . . he groped for the right word. Hurt. He was hurt and wounded. Rallus wanted to put laughter in the man's eyes. He wanted to do a lot of things to him.

He watched Knox kneeling on the floor, lighting a new candle.

Phhht.

That was weird. A second candle blew out. Rallus dropped to the floor and took charge of it as a third candle extinguished itself.

Rallus grinned. "The old man is trying to keep me away from you. He's jealous."

They lit the candles and met, on their knees by the dead man's feet. "No, I don't think that's it."

This time, Knox needed no urging. They kissed with a raw hunger until Rallus stood and drew Knox to his feet beside him. Knox gasped when Rallus took him into his arms.

They tried to keep their kisses quiet, but it was difficult. When Rallus unbuttoned Knox's jeans, he smiled when he felt the hard cock waiting for him.

"A treasure," he whispered and bent to lick it.

Knox kept his mouth closed, but Rallus heard the low groan in his throat as he knelt before him and took possession of Knox's cock with his mouth. He sucked slowly at first until his own need made him suck harder, faster.

No, he had something else in mind.

Knox's brows knitted in bewilderment. He wasn't resistant anymore but seemed surprised when Rallus pushed him over the table, then bent down and started licking and sucking his ass.

"Oh!" Knox choked off the exclamation and buried his face in the polished wood table as Rallus swabbed his ass with his hot tongue.

Rallus unbuckled his belt, unzipped his jeans, and released his own cock.

Knox reached behind him to feel it, and his fingers found the grand prize.

"I knew you'd be huge," he whispered. "Oh God, Rallus . . ."

Rallus's face plunged back into Knox's ass. He held the man's hips up to his face and then straightened. He used his hard cock in feather-light strokes across Knox's ass. Down his crack, between those sweet cheeks, across the backs of Knox's thighs, he allowed more pressure, leaving a warm sticky trail.

Knox chewed off his arrested moans.

Rallus reached between Knox's parted thighs and toyed with his balls, down to his cock, jerking gently on it. He grunted and planted his tongue at Knox's ass hole again.

Both men felt the flash-fire ignite. Rallus couldn't wait. He flipped Knox over on his back. At the same moment, he wondered what would happen if Mrs. King walked in now. He grabbed Knox's straining cock and engulfed it in one swift movement.

Knox came hard, his hips moving up from the table, his arms flopping to his sides, a packet of candles falling to the floor.

"Oh . . ." Knox's face registered fear and pleasure in his moments of release. "You . . . you didn't come." His fingers reached for Rallus's cock.

"No, baby. That's a sixty-eight. You owe me one."

Another candle on the floor extinguished.

Rallus glanced at the body and smirked. "Get your own guy, Harold."

Adrian drove down North Shore Drive, startled to see Rallus coming out of the Lakeside Funeral Home. He was stunned, and he was furious. He watched him walk along the street and disappear around the corner.

Ah, so he lives around here. He sighed and reached into his pocket for the number again. There it was, the purple building. With the phones still out in the town, he hadn't been able to call and confirm his appointment with the psychic reader.

His friend Jen swore by Sandy.

"She's good. Don't let her talk you into buying candles and crystals or anything. Just go for the reading; she's great."

He sighed. He had no idea why he was so nervous. Jen said getting a reading was like getting a spiritual massage. Adrian reminded himself of this. Yet he felt a cold dread that had nothing to do with the weather outside or his toasty vehicle. He parked, locked up, and walked over to the front door. He was about to knock when he heard loud voices from inside.

"I want stuffed cabbage!" a young boy was screaming.

"Mikey, what are you talking about? You hate cabbage," a woman's voice said. She sounded weary.

"I want cabbage soup. And potato latkes. None of this . . . meshugas . . ."

"What did he say?" a man's voice piped up.

"I have no idea." The woman sounded dispirited. "Mikey . . . darling . . . please. You love Frosted Flakes."

"No, I don't."

"Yes, you do."

The man's voice roared over both of theirs. "Michael, eat your cereal, or I'll give you a thrashing you'll never forget."

"See here," the little boy said, and his voice sounded hard . . . weird. "You touch me . . . .you . . . you . . ." The child's voice drifted, then rang out in confident tones, "I'll call Child Protective Services."

"You'll . . . what?"

"You heard. You touch me again, I'll tell the police everything I know."

The woman broke into sobs. "Michael!"

Adrian stood back from the door when he heard the movement of feet. He jumped out of the way and flattened himself against the wall of the building, but the feet went into the opposite direction.

He heard the woman shout as the child ran out of the building and onto the street. He saw a dark-haired boy in jeans and a sweater. The kid turned and stared at Adrian and with a weird, chilling smirk, crossed the road and ran toward the lake.

Adrian heard the couple arguing.

"What does he know, Sandy?" the husband asked as they came out of the building. "What has he heard?"

Adrian shrank against the wall.

"He's heard everything. He listened when Mel was here."

Mel. Adrian's thoughts flew. He walked briskly away from the building as the couple ran across the road after their son. He blew out a sigh. Mel. Was it the Mel he knew? He walked back to his car, thankful he'd arrived when he had. He wadded up the piece of paper with Sandy's contact information. That was two hundred dollars he'd just saved himself.

Rallus returned to his log cabin home, struck anew at how picture-perfect it was. Perfect on the outside, a house of everyday horrors inside. He parked the truck and slipped through the back door. It felt like home . . . sometimes. Until he opened the cupboards.

He sighed. Chances were good that he'd be bringing Knox home. The small ripple of pleasure . . . of hope, replaced the emptiness he'd felt.

He had to clean the place up. Sure, it had been part of the agreement but—he held his hand to the first cupboard.

"Come in," he said, startling the woman peering over his kitchen window.

Penny's face fully emerged over the frosted glass. At least she had the grace to look guilty.

He opened the door to the blast of mountain chill.

"I don't believe we've met." He held out his hand. She took it, and her fingers trembled in his powerful grip.

"My name is Rallus. And you are?"

"Penny." Her voice squeaked. "Penny Tresean."

He heard a long, low whine from outside.

"That's my dog, Phoenix." She looked both hopeful and a little afraid.

"Come, Phoenix," he called out, and the dog dashed in like a furry bullet. Rallus closed the door behind her, the dog's tail whipping at his ankles.

Rallus opened a cupboard and withdrew a bowl. "I don't have a dog dish."

He poured water into it and placed it on the floor beside Phoenix who gave it a dutiful lick but kept watching him as if Rallus was going to turn up something much better than tap water.

"Now that you're here, Penny, perhaps you can explain this."

Rallus opened a cupboard to reveal dozens and dozens of cans all lined up on shelves. They were all one brand and appeared to be soups and pasta sauces.

"I . . . I don't understand," she said.

He held up a finger.

"They're all empty. Why in the world would anyone line up a bunch of clean, washed and empty cans like this? Is this a Fawnskin thing?"

She reached out and hesitated. "May I?"

"Be my guest."

Penny took a can, and sure enough, the lid had been closed, but it was empty.

Rallus sighed. "I've been trying to figure it out for three days."

Penny glanced from him to the stack of boxes in the living room.

"The Lensons know you're here?"

He frowned at her. "Of course. What did you . . . oh!" He snapped his fingers. "You thought I was an intruder."

Phoenix lapped noisily at the water as if reminding them both that she was still there.

"I don't have anything for you, Phoenix," Rallus said, reaching down and stroking the dog's head. "Sorry."

"Wow," Penny said. "She never lets anyone touch her. I'm shocked."

"Dogs love me. I attract 'em. Dogs and empty cans."

"I think I can explain the cans."

Rallus arched a brow in her direction.

"Mrs. Lenson survived the Depression. She was frugal . . . ridiculously so. She never wanted people to think she wasn't doing well. I didn't realize she was still doing this."

She gestured at the cans. "I thought her family had filled it with actual food . . ." Her voice drifted away.

Rallus began emptying the cans into a garbage bin.

"How long are you staying?"

"I don't know."

"A man of mystery."

He smiled. "You have any idea who might want a bunch of empty cans for recycling, or should I just leave them with the trash?"

She shook her head. "Holy moly this place is filled with . . . dolls."

"Tell me about it."

"What are you going to do with them?"

"I think the family wants to sell them. I took it on short notice. I—"

He broke off, resentful to be revealing so much. He'd made it clear that he wanted peace and privacy. He'd not only managed to bed two guys, he now had a nosy neighbor poking through his things. He watched Penny moving around the living room.

"I see tissue here. Are you supposed to wrap the dolls?"

He nodded.

"I can do that." She checked her watch. "I've got time for at least a box or two."

He glanced at her. He fought the urge to tell her to fuck off and go home, but she was already taping up the bottom of a box, and he did want to see the back of all those creepy dolls.

"You got a radio?" she asked.

"I've got an iPod."

"Cool."

She moved to the docking station across the room, and Glen Miller let them know he was In the Mood.

"I'll make coffee," Rallus said over the music.

Penny glanced up from a box and smiled. Phoenix raised a hopeful head from her paws on the floor.

"Not for you, Phoenix." He smiled at the dog's sad expression. "Next time, I'll give you chicken."

As soon as Rallus left with a promise to return, Knox tried relighting the candles. This time they all stayed lit. Knox sat cross-legged on the floor next to Harold. He studied the shrouded body for several moments before speaking. "Okay. It's time you and I had a talk."

For some unknown reason, he waited a few beats in case

Harold had something to say. When he realized what he'd done he let out a snort and shook his head. *I'm going insane.*

"I'm trying to figure out how you can be inside Michael, yet still be here enough to fuck with the candles. And for that matter, why a boy? If it was me and I could possess someone, it would be someone who got to do the things I hadn't been able to in my later life. Like . . . me or Rallus."

A thought struck him. "Is that what the little tantrum with the candles was all about? Were you disgusted by Rallus giving me the best damn rimming of my life or were you jealous?"

A knock at the door startled him. He sat up straighter and turned to see Mrs. King peeking in.

"Sorry. I thought I heard voices."

Knox watched as Mrs. King's nose twitched like she smelled something faintly familiar in the air. He bit the inside of his cheek to keep from smiling. "Sorry. I've been spending so much time with Mr. Herxheimer I've started talking to him without thinking."

Mrs. King gave him a disapproving stare. "Well, I've come to relieve you for a spell. There's fried chicken in the kitchen."

At the announcement of food, Knox's stomach grumbled. "Homemade?"

Mrs. King looked at him like he was crazy. "Of course it's homemade."

Knox stood, embarrassed. He couldn't remember ever eating chicken that hadn't come out of a bucket. His mom hadn't exactly been the domestic type. He walked by Mrs. King and smiled. "I'm sorry. I meant no offense."

Mrs. King's face softened. "Don't you worry about it. I made extra, so help yourself to whatever you want."

Knox didn't need any further coaxing. He left the room and followed the smell of chicken to the kitchen. The countertop was laden with more food than he'd ever seen. Not only had the kind woman made chicken, but mashed potatoes, green beans, rolls, and there was some kind of fruity marshmallow salad.

Knox almost fell to his knees in praise for the gifts he was about to receive. He grabbed a plate and piled on as much food as it would hold. Sitting at the table, he poured a large glass of lemonade. His hands shook as he lifted the crispy, golden piece of chicken to his mouth.

The first taste sent shivers up his spine, his teeth biting through the crunchy outer layer to the moist dark meat inside. Oh fuck. He was surprised to realize tears had come to his eyes. You're so pathetic, Knox.

He couldn't be too hard on himself. For months he'd barely managed to scrounge a bite of food every couple of days. It had been his choice though, he needed to remember that.

After leaving behind the rather seedy lifestyle he'd once lived, he'd been left with nothing but his car . . . and Curtis. He'd tried so hard to keep his Schnauzer-Labrador mix with him, but it had been unfair to Curtis. His parents had a yard, something his faithful companion deserved.

He scooped up a large bite of the buttery potatoes and moaned as they hit his taste buds. She may be nosy and a little strange, but damn could Mrs. King cook.

Commotion outside the kitchen window caught his attention. Not willing to leave his plate, he picked it up and carried it over to the sink as he continued eating. The plate wobbled in his grasp as he stared into the face of the boy he'd rescued earlier.

His appetite forgotten for the moment, Knox set the plate on the counter just as Sandy rounded the corner of the funeral home shouting Michael's name. She stopped beside him and dropped to her knees, wrapping her arms around her son.

Michael gave no inclination that he even noticed the woman or her hold on him. He continued to stare up at Knox. Sandy eventually followed her son's gaze and seemed shocked.

Knox put his hand on the cold glass. Michael, in turn, held his palm toward the window. Gooseflesh broke out on Knox's skin as he witnessed the unspoken cry for help.

He swallowed around the lump in his throat as Sandy picked up her son. She gave Knox one last questioning glance before carrying Michael away.

Was that really Michael, or Harold? Knox didn't know the answer, but he felt it was Michael. When they'd found the boy near the cemetery earlier, he seemed more in control, sure of himself. At the time, Harold had spoken to him through the boy.

Knox glanced over his shoulder toward the door that led to the room that held Mr. Herxheimer's corpse. If Michael was out there, then Harold must be back in his body, but why?

He stuffed as much chicken into his mouth as he could manage without choking and went to find out.

When he entered the room, Mrs. King was standing over the body. The room smelled of incense, and several of the candles were once again extinguished.

"Is everything okay?" he asked.

Mrs. King's face was pale. "You haven't left Mr. Herxheimer alone have you?"

Fuck! No way could he tell the older woman the truth. He needed the money the job provided. "No. Why?"

Mrs. King looked back down at the shrouded body. "Just making sure."

He could tell by her expression that she didn't believe him. Did she know about Harold running around town in Michael's body? Knox decided to change the subject, afraid for his job.

"That was the best dinner I've had in years. Thank you so much."

Mrs. King's expression changed to one of pride. "You're welcome. I used to love to cook for my family, but now that Lionel has passed and Jason is married . . ." She waved her hand in a dismissive motion. "Anyway, it's nice to have someone to cook for."

"Well, feel free to cook for me anytime." He chuckled, trying to lighten the mood.

After one last glance at the body, she turned and walked toward the door. "Oh. Did you need to use the restroom before I go?"

Knox didn't, but he knew it would be better to at least attempt to empty his bladder. "Yes. Thank you."

He quickly left the room and entered the bathroom. Guilt was starting to really set in. Because of his need to pee, he'd not only cursed Mr. Herxheimer but an innocent child.

Knox knew it was up to him to set things right. And just how the hell do I do that?

Penny was a godsend. She was not as snoopy as a lot of women Rallus knew, and she wrapped and packed three boxes of dolls with a minimum of conversation. The music had stopped, and she'd been quick to select new albums on his iPod, but as he glanced into the living room, he saw her standing in the middle of the room holding a dark-haired baby doll in her hand. Her other hand trembled at her mouth. He noticed her slim, gold wedding band at the same moment her face scrunched into a terrible expression of anguish.

Gawd, is she crying?

He paused. He'd been about to offer her more coffee. He

looked away as she glanced at him. He averted his gaze, giving her a few seconds to compose herself. When he glanced back, she'd turned her face, hiding her tears.

The doll in her hands lay on its back, its little arms arched upward. Did she want a baby? Was that the problem? Boy, had she come to the wrong guy. He returned to his task, and when he looked over at her again, she seemed to be unable to wrap the doll, in spite of her repeated attempts.

How . . . weird.

He watched her pick it up twice and put it back down again. She seemed agonized. He felt her grief. That's what it was. It was almost as if the doll was a living, breathing child and she couldn't bring herself to pack it in the box.

Rallus was on the verge of telling Penny to keep the doll. Something stopped him. He recognized in her a similarly wounded soul. Some of us show our wounds . . . some of us carry them in our souls . . . some of us are waiting for them to overtake our bodies.

They both jumped when they heard the voice outside.

"Penny?"

She blinked and frowned.

"Penny?"

"Pop?" She brushed past her little worktable and went to the front door. Rallus followed her as she opened it. An elderly man stood there, and Rallus saw the look of shock on her face.

"Oh . . . oh, Pop. You're walking!"

"Of course I'm walking. What kind of meshuga talk is this?"

Penny looked astonished. "Pop?"

The elderly man stood at the door, Phoenix greeting him with noisy yaps and much tail whipping. The smile fell from the old man's face as he looked beyond Penny across the room. "Antonio?"

Penny turned, her face twisted in pain again. "No, no . . ." She gazed at Rallus. "Please. Please, take the doll."

"I don't understand," Rallus said. "I—"

"Antonio!" The elderly man stumbled toward the baby doll. "Antonio." The sound from his heart tore at Rallus as Penny's father held it to his chest, great, racking sobs spewed from him. "My baby boy . . . .my baby boy." Tears fell down his face. "Look, Penny, I found our boy."

Penny began to cry, covering her face with her hands.

Rallus put his arms around her. She leaned into him, and he was surprised how thin she was under the thick sweaters she wore.

"He looks like my son," she said. "He looks just like Antonio."

Her father moved to the sofa and held the doll as if to pacify a crying infant. From somewhere he produced a baby bottle and popped it into the doll's mouth.

"Oh, my God," Penny moaned, pushing herself away from Rallus.

"Penny," Rallus began.

"He was killed. My baby was killed a year ago. He was three weeks old. He was killed in an accident with my husband and my daughter. That . . . that doll looks just like him."

"Oh, Penny . . . I am so sorry."

She stared at her father, who looked up at her.

"Shhh, Penny, baby's sleeping," he said and leaned back into the sofa and closed his eyes.

Penny clutched her stomach as if she were in mortal agony.

"When does it stop?" She gasped. "When does it stop hurting all the fucking time?"

"I don't know," Rallus said putting his arm around her.

Her words came out in a rush. "The baby couldn't sleep.

He was so beautiful, but he wasn't like Luisa. And you know, people say it's usually girls who fuss, but Luisa was a wonderful girl. God! I miss them so much. Johnny, my husband . . . he took the baby for a drive so he could sleep. I was exhausted. I shouldn't have let them go."

"Oh, don't blame yourself. Please, Penny, that's not fair."

He was certain she'd been told this many times, but she plunged ahead.

"Luisa loved the baby and wanted to go, too, and . . . and . . . they were killed. A drunk driver. Hit them head-on. I lost them all."

She swatted at her tears, shrugged Rallus's comforting arm from her shoulders. She straightened now. "I can't believe my father walked here."

Penny gazed at her father and said, "What's a meshuga?"

Rallus stood, confused.

"My father, when he came in, he said, meshuga."

"Oh, it's Yiddish. It means nonsense."

She gaped at him. "Yiddish? I wonder how he learned a word like that." Penny moved toward her father and tried to take the doll from him.

"Let him keep it," Rallus said. "The Lensons won't miss it. I'll let them know we're keeping one."

Penny's hand dropped to the baby doll's brow, and she stroked it gently. "There isn't one that looks like Luisa. I looked." She started to cry again.

It was odd how limp Michael was, how he'd just passed out in her arms like a rag doll. When she walked in the door, she was dismayed to find Steve there. She thought he'd gone off drinking. She'd even taken some of the money from her stash and given it to him, hoping he'd disappear for a few days.

"That brat wander off again?"

"He's all right, Steve, leave him alone," she said, taking the baby quickly into the other room. She laid him gently in his bed, touching his head. "He won't hurt you. I won't let him. I promise."

She needed an angle, a client with money. She needed to focus. That big, dark hunk who'd brought home Michael . . . she wondered about him. What was his story? All she needed to do was focus, and that could be a very lucrative situation. One more big score and then she was getting out of here, her and Michael, away from that bastard forever.

Knox sat there staring at the sheet that shrouded Mr. Herxheimer's body, almost willing it to move. "What is it you want with me? Okay, I messed up. I took a pee, okay? But leave that kid alone. He didn't do anything to you."

Dybbuk. He wanted to tell Rallus about it, but Rallus would think he was out of his mind. He hadn't believed it even when Mrs. King talked about it, but he did now.

"Talk to me, Harold. Are you there, or are you somewhere else?"

Silence.

"Play with the damn candles then. Do something. I'm losing my mind. And do you have to be so damn creepy inside that kid? I'm sorry if you know . . . me and Rallus put on a show for you and all. You seemed upset. I know . . . probably disrespectful."

Better with the lights off, that's all. Gawd, I may be dead, but I'm not a prude.

Knox jumped up from where he sat on the sofa. "Did you say that, or am I imagining it?"

"Talking to ghosts?" a voice said suddenly.

Knox turned around, breathless, relaxing when he saw

the tall outline of Rallus standing in the doorway. He smiled. "No, I . . . hi." He couldn't help but smile. The guy was beautiful.

"Hi. I came for a kiss."

"Only a kiss?"

He laughed. "'For starters."

"We can't do that in front of . . . him." Knox hooked his thumb toward the body.

"Why?" Rallus reached out and grabbed him.

Knox laughed, and all the candles went out at the same time. "Whoa!"

Rallus moved his lips against his cheek. "Don't worry about it. It's better in the dark."

Knox pushed away from him. "Now you're freaking me out. He just said that."

"Who just said what?"

"Harold."

"Why are you halfway across the room now?" Rallus seemed frustrated. He searched around blindly for something to light the candles with.

"Okay, I'm just going to say it. Do you know what a dybbuk is?"

"Do I know what a what is?" He managed to light one candle. He was staring at him strangely.

Knox grabbed the matches out of his hand and lit another candle. "It's a Jewish custom which says that you have to watch the dead at all times or they walk."

"Walk where exactly?" He was grinning.

"Don't be smart. They . . . okay, I took a pee, and he decided to find a body."

"Huh?"

"I didn't do my job. I had to pee. You're not supposed to leave them five minutes, and I did, and then Harold went into that little boy, but I don't know why?"

"You really believe that."

"Yes, I do. Didn't you think that kid was acting well . . . bizarre?"

Rallus seemed to consider that. "Yeah. I guess he was."

"Remember you told me you thought that something was going on?"

"Yeah, you mean about abuse?"

"Yes. I think you're right. I think somehow Harold is trying to help, maybe protect him in his own way."

Rallus said nothing. He just stared at him.

"Harold," Knox whispered. "Am I right? Do we need to help Michael?"

Nothing.

"Well, Harold isn't talking. How long before you can get out of here, take a break?"

"You have something in mind?" He smiled.

"I didn't even get the lousy kiss."

Knox smiled. "Rallus, you do believe me, don't you, about Harold?"

He sighed. "Let me digest it, okay?"

"Okay."

"I'll tell you what . . . Let's look into it, go to Michael's school tomorrow."

Knox nodded. "Okay. Good idea."

CHAPTER FIVE

Adrian slipped into the booth at the Route 62 Old Timer Diner off the 10 Freeway. It was out of the way, about forty minutes from Fawnskin with the ice and minimum visibility on the freeway, but this place was worth it.

He picked up the plastic laminated menu and studied it. Just for kicks, he checked to see if they still had the twenty-thousand-dollar burger listed. Yep, he was relieved some things didn't change. The burger came with a free, brand-new Harley. One day he might just buy that burger. He itched to go out back and check out the Harley dealership that was part of the place. It was filled with antique Harleys.

"Coffee?" the middle-aged sweet-faced waitress asked him.

He nodded. Sunderman was late as usual. He checked his watch. By the time he glanced back up again, his lanky boss was striding toward him.

Oh man, get a load of this outfit. Jeans, boots, western shirt, a belt buckle the size of a frickin' dinner plate.

Sunderman always dressed this way when he came out west.

He slid into the booth opposite Adrian and eyed the provocatively-placed pies on the bar top.

"Hey, sugar," the waitress said. "Can I get you some coffee?"

"Sure."

She filled his cup. "Warm yours up?" she asked Adrian, waiting a fraction of a second before pouring.

"I'll have chicken fried steak," Sunderman told her. "It's the best in the world here."

She smiled with the assurance of one who's been told this countless times.

Adrian cast another glance at the twenty-thousand-dollar burger and opted for a less expensive one, plus fries and onion rings.

They waited until she was gone. Adrian toyed with his placemat, filled with biker lingo. The Old Timer Diner promised to rev your engine with its shakes and pies.

"How did it go?"

Adrian glanced up at Sunderman. "Fine. Nobody's suspicious. I said I was . . ." He broke off, his thoughts returning to the incredible night of passion he'd shared with Rallus. He squirmed, thinking of the guy's tongue on his skin.

"They think I'm an architect. I've—"

Sunderman butted in. "But you've made contact with the subject."

Adrian's eyes glittered. He felt bad now. He'd never felt guilty before on an assignment, but this time he did. A bank president filing a huge insurance payment on a two-million-dollar suspicious, nighttime robbery was a big deal, especially in this economy.

He blew out a sigh. "If Mel Gower had anything to do with the robbery, he's got nothing to show for it. His bar is falling down around his ears. He's a man under a lot of stress."

Adrian paused, but for some reason couldn't bring himself to sip his coffee. It bothered him to see a nice guy like Mel the target of an insurance investigation. The cops had already arrested Mel's ex-lover, Nick Brash, for the theft. If they didn't think they had enough evidence to implicate Mel as having worked with Brash on the theft, why did his employer insist he did? Oh, yeah, that insipid bank manager,

Cantor. He's the one who'd put the bug in Sunderman's ear about Mel being guilty.

"I can almost guarantee you Mel doesn't have the bank money."

"How do you know? According to the bank's manager, Mel and Nick Brash were inseparable at the time of the robbery."

Adrian shrugged. "I don't. It's just a feeling. I've done this job long enough to know when to follow my gut instinct, and I'm telling you, Mel had nothing to do with that robbery."

He thought about the conversation they'd had, how Mel yearned to fix up his bar, but couldn't.

"I'd say whatever went down with Mel and Brash is in the past." Of course Nick Brash was currently sitting in jail awaiting trial.

"Stay on him. You know that Cantor claims Mel has it out for him. That Mel, in fact, told him on several occasions that the interest the bank was charging on his loan, he'd be better off just robbing the place to pay it back."

The waitress came out with their meals. How she managed to juggle the dishes and that hot pot of coffee was a mystery to Adrian. He waited until she'd topped up their cups and swished away in her white, orthopedic shoes before continuing.

"I realize that. But I think it's Cantor who has it out for Mel, not the other way around. The guy wouldn't even look me in the eyes when I questioned him about his claims. Several times I got the feeling he was almost jealous of Mel and Brash's relationship."

Sunderson forked some mashed potatoes. "Don't forget, Cantor's a married man. A straight, married man."

Adrian rolled his eyes. Like that ever stopped anyone.

Sunderson began making notes in a small book. Adrian

hated that book. He hated his part in this. Being an under-cover insurance investigator could be fun when he was fol-lowing allegedly crippled celebrities all over ski slopes in Europe. This—what was happening to Mel—felt wrong. It felt very cruel.

"I'll stay on it," he said aloud and picked up his thick burger and took a chomp out of it.

Nobody was home when Knox and Rallus went to call on Michael and his parents. It was probably just as well. Knox looked exhausted, and he had a scant five hours before he was due back corpse-watching at the funeral parlor. He needed sleep. Rallus preferred not to go right across the road to the cabin room Knox was staying in for privacy's sake. So he suggested his place.

Knox was quiet on the short drive, admiring the lake and huge, snow-kissed trees when they arrived.

"Somebody likes soup," Knox said when he spotted the many boxes filled with them, lined outside the back door.

"Long story," Rallus said with a laugh. He was genuinely pleased to have Knox here. It felt . . . right.

"You like dolls?" Knox asked as he walked past the kitch-en and into the living room.

There was a knock on the kitchen door, and Penny poked her head around the corner. She had a covered plate in her hands. So much for privacy.

"Hi, Rallus." She saw Knox and her face lit up. "Hi, Knox."

"You two know each other?" Rallus asked.

"Yes, we met at the funeral home," Knock said. "She bakes a mean cookie."

Penny grinned. "I baked more and thought I'd bring you some."

"Wow, thanks," Rallus said and lifted a cookie from under the mountain of foil. He held it up. "It's a man."

"Oh . . ." Knox sounded as if he was groaning. "It's Mr. Herxheimer."

"Mr. Herxheimer, eh?" Rallus was tickled. "Chocolate-dipped, too." He took a bite. "Very good."

Penny beamed.

"How's your dad doing?" he asked her.

"Oh, he's okay. No idea where that burst of energy came from. He can't walk at all now. He's back in his wheelchair. Thanks for letting him keep the doll . . . and thanks for helping me get him home."

"No problem."

"I gotta get going. Mrs. King wants these cookies for the afternoon viewing. There's been another death up at the retirement home. She's gonna have her hands full tonight."

She left, and Rallus shut the door.

"You want to eat?"

"No." Knox pressed himself into Rallus's arms. "I want to go to bed with you."

"You won't get any arguments from me."

The two men kissed.

"I probably need to shower and brush my teeth," Knox said.

"Hey, I can help you out there."

Rallus went into the bathroom and came out with a new toothbrush. "My furnace finally kicked in. It's been heating up for two days. Wanna have a bath with me?"

"Sure," Knox said.

Knox cleaned his teeth around Rallus who spent time running the tub with potions and oils and bubbly stuff that smelled like lavender.

Rallus massaged Knox's shoulders until he felt the tension easing. The two men undressed and Rallus felt his equilibri-

um and his erection coming back as they sank into the
foamy water. His hands moved all over Knox's legs and
thighs, sliding up to his cock and balls.

Knox glanced around the bathroom. "It's an old lady's
place. You just move in or something?"

"Yep. Part of the deal is I clean it up."

"What's this?" Knox went toward the towel rack and
pulled off the black fabric Rallus had used as a blindfold on
Adrian.

"Nothing."

"Looks like a blindfold to me."

Rallus stared at him.

"I've been with my share of kinky guys." Knox looked ten
years older in that moment.

"Yes, I'm sure you have."

"You might as well know I've had a crappy life. I'm trying to change that."

"I'm glad you are." Rallus's hand moved back up to
Knox's cock. He held it in his warm, soapy hands and kissed
the ripening head peeking through the suds.

Knox moaned again.

"I want to fuck you," Rallus said.

"Yeah, I want that, too."

Lust hovered in a gentle haze over Knox's eyes.

"You're so beautiful," Rallus said and pulled Knox into
his arms. Their kiss went deep and became more impassioned.

Rallus picked him up and carried him to the bedroom, the
sudden chill adding an extra, thrilling spark.

Neither man said a word as Rallus stripped back the bedding and they slipped, still wet, into the sheets. He knelt between Knox's open thighs and their cocks rubbed against
one another as they tongue danced.

Knox moaned. "Fuck me."

Rallus reached for a rubber and knocked over the entire bedside table. A gun was taped to the back of it, which surprised him. It was a serious gun, not an old lady's little cap gun.

"Hurry," Knox said into his shoulder, and Rallus grabbed a fresh rubber. The heat between the two men kept his breath coming in short, sharp bursts.

He lapped at Knox's ass briefly. He was too far gone to do more than that. He had to have him. Now.

"Oh, God . . ." Knox thrashed around the bed and Rallus skewered him with his meaty cock.

He rammed into Knox, loving the feel of him. Oh . . . this is better than Adrian . . . this is better than . . . anybody. Why did I have to meet him now?

Knox and Rallus were perfectly matched. Thrust for thrust, the two men gave and received every ounce of pleasure they could. Knox grabbed Rallus's ass cheeks as if keeping him in place, pulling him closer, tighter . . . harder and his ass muscles clamped down on Rallus's cock. They came together, hard, biting and sucking at each other's mouths.

"That was—"

Rallus smiled when his hot little lover fell asleep in his arms, mid-sentence.

"Yeah," he said, kissing Knox's warm brow. "Yeah, baby . . . it was."

Knox stretched, feeling the warm body pressed against his back. He glanced at his watch and sighed. If only he could lie in Rallus's arms another ten hours . . . or ten years. He grinned. Wouldn't that just freak Rallus the hell out?

He flipped back the covers and tried to get out of bed without waking his new lover, but Rallus evidently had other plans. A strong arm pulled Knox right back against Rallus's muscled chest.

"Where do you think you're sneaking off to?" Rallus finished the question with a nip to Knox's neck.

"I need to be at work in a little over an hour. I didn't want to wake you, so I thought I'd just walk."

Rallus turned Knox so they were face-to-face. "Don't be ridiculous. It's fucking freezing out there."

Knox stared into Rallus's dark eyes while running a finger over his plump brown lips. Had he ever had a lover who gave a shit whether he walked home? Knox knew he wasn't nearly good enough for such special treatment. What was it about Rallus that made him want to confess his sins?

"You're a better man than I deserve," he finally admitted.

"Bullshit."

Knox shook his head. "There are things about me that you don't know."

"You ever killed someone?"

Knox's chest squeezed painfully. "I tried to kill myself once. Does that count?"

Rallus's black brows knitted together. "No. How long ago?"

"Three months, one week and four days." Knox bit his bottom lip. He wasn't sure how far he could go in explaining his life without completely turning Rallus off. "I've been on my own for a long time. Like most kids who leave home too early, I had to do a lot of things I'm not proud of."

Rallus leaned in and gave Knox a soft kiss. "What you had to do doesn't reflect who you are now."

Knox tried his best to smile. "I'm trying to get my life back on track. I've been living in my car for the last few months, but at least I got away . . ."

Rallus kissed Knox again, this time deeper. "Whatever it was that brought you to Fawnskin, I'm glad."

"Thanks."

Knox was hungry when he walked in the door. Of course, he was always hungry when it came to this place. That woman could cook up a storm. He got right to work digging into a savory stew as Mrs. King watched silently.

"Aren't you joining me?" he asked, pausing in between bites.

"No. I ate earlier. Enjoy, enjoy. Mr. Herxheimer will be going to his final resting place tomorrow, so tonight is your last night together. Benjamin Mandelstamm joins him tonight, and then you'll be watching him."

"They'll be together then?"

"Yes. Funny really, Harold didn't like anyone, especially not Benjamin." She chuckled. "He was a malcontent."

"Who? Harold, or Benjamin?"

"Harold of course."

"Was he a criminal?"

"No. He was a lawyer. Same difference some say," she muttered.

"Was he ah . . . very spiritual kind of person, deeply religious?"

"Hell no. He went through the motions like a lot of folk. Why you ask?"

"No reason."

"I wanted to tell you, don't you be worrying about your job now. Looks like you'll be staying on here for a while. They seem to be dropping like flies at the Jewish Elder Care Center."

When she'd left the kitchen, Knox contemplated his new charge. He had no idea what this would mean as far as Harold was concerned. Probably he wouldn't be wandering around anymore. Anyway, he had no intention of letting the new guy wander. He wouldn't leave the room if it killed him, and he was bringing a bottle with him to pee in.

He was daydreaming about Rallus when he heard the doorbell ring. Rallus was a mystery, which was probably part of his appeal, big, dark and mysterious, with a real gun taped to the back of his nightstand. What in hell was that about? He still didn't know what it was that Rallus did for a living, but he seemed to be on vacation or something.

He stood up when the hearse brought the corpse in. He nodded to the guy on his way out and walked into the room just in time to see Mrs. King covering the body.

"Get some more candles," she told him, "and place them around."

Knox lit three candles and walked around, putting them down strategically.

Mrs. King left him soon after, and he walked around the room, studying the two corpses lying side by side. "So, you didn't like each other eh? Ironic, how you ended up in the same place." A breeze blew through the room suddenly, and two of the candles went out.

"Okay, don't be so sensitive," he joked. "I didn't mean anything by it." He relit the candles. He sat down nearby and closed his eyes. "Don't go to sleep. Don't go to sleep." He could see Rallus, naked, hard, standing there in front of him, and he moaned inwardly.

Don't you ever think of anything else? Geez.

Knox's eyes snapped open. "Harold? Is that you?"

Who do you think it is, your mother?

"Harold, I wish I could figure you out."

Figure out that hunk you've been humping. He's closer than you think.

"What do you mean, closer to what?"

There was no answer, just the wind.

When he heard a small voice call out, "Mr. Herxheimer," he just about jumped out of his skin. He thought he'd imagined it, but there was a loud tapping at the window.

He approached the window with trepidation, only relaxing when he saw Michael staring up at him. "What are you doing here?"

"Let me in."

"Come around to the front; the door is open." Knox screwed up his face. What was he doing here at this time of night?

When Knox opened the door to the room, Michael walked right past him and over to the corpse. "Mr. Herxheimer," he said, "I'm here."

Knox pulled him back from the corpse. "Michael. How do you know his name? Are you afraid of him? Has he hurt you?"

Michael shrugged away from him. "He's going to kill him for me," he replied, but his gaze never wavered from the corpse. He put up his hands.

"Michael, no!" Knox said, shaking his head. "He's leaving. He's going tomorrow, he's—"

"No," Michael said suddenly, looking up at him, "he's not. He's not going anywhere until it's over."

"Until what's over?"

Suddenly, the voice which answered him had changed, deepened. "You'll see. They'll all see."

"Harold, please," Knox pleaded. "Don't hurt the boy."

"I'm all he has. He knows that. Ah, here she comes." He smiled.

When Sandy burst into the room, she was incensed, accusing Knox of all kinds of things.

"Listen to me, he's not himself. He's someone else."

"What in hell is wrong with you? You on drugs? I know you been fucking that tall cool drink of water. I know what you are. Don't you touch my boy!"

"Her boy!" Michael laughed hysterically. "Her boy!"

"What is going on in here?" Mrs. King burst into the room. "Don't you have any respect for the dead? Knox, what is this . . ." Her eyes widened, and she gazed over at the two corpses. "Get out," she said absently to the mother and her son. "Leave now."

"Gladly," Sandy sputtered. "Just lucky I don't report you weirdoes to the authorities."

Sandy was gone, dragging her son with her. Mrs. King was desperately trying to light the candles which continued to go out as soon as they were lit. "He's gone, isn't he?" She turned to Knox, her hand over her mouth now.

"Who?"

"You know who? What happened? You left him. You left him"

"I had to pee." That excuse sounded lame at the moment.

Mrs. King paced the floor. She mumbled over and over to herself in Yiddish and then stopped and stared at him. "How long have you known?"

"Since Michael disappeared."

"And you didn't tell me?"

"I . . ." He lowered his head.

"What's that boy got to do with this?"

"Mr. Herxheimer has possessed the boy. He wants to help him because . . ."

"Herxheimer wouldn't help anyone in life. What makes you think he's changed? Besides, that's not what happens. The reason the dead attach themselves to the living is to fix something for themselves, not for others. They don't run away becoming crusaders for justice. He's using the boy, that's all."

Knox sighed. "Could he hurt him?"

"He could get him to hurt himself. I never thought I'd see the day again."

"What do you mean by again?"

"I made the same mistake a few years ago. I fell asleep while watching a corpse, and when I awoke, he was gone. He caused a lot of havoc, and finally, he just moved on when it was over. But you can never tell what they're up to."

"I suppose I've lost my job."

"No, you haven't lost your job. I need you to watch this one, and I need you to find Harold Herxheimer. You did this, now you fix it. And whatever you do, don't tell the family."

Her nerves were fried, and she'd let her temper get the best of her when she put Michael to bed. "Why are you always wandering over there to that funeral home?"

"Maybe I'm obsessed with death."

Those big words. How did such a little boy suddenly develop a vocabulary like that? He'd changed so much, and not in a good way. He was definite and sarcastic. He seemed to have an answer for everything. "That guy over there is not a good person to hang out with. I don't want you with him."

"Why, because he likes cock?"

Her eyes widened. "Where did you hear that?"

"Nowhere. He doesn't like little cocks, Mother dear, just really, really big ones."

"Enough of that. No more talking to that man. You see what happens."

He laughed. "Let me sleep, will you?"

She had gone outside, smoked several cigarettes and wondered if she was suddenly in some kind of nightmare. She knew that stranger was boinking the dark-haired one. The dark-haired one had money. Maybe he wouldn't want anyone to know that he was one of those faggot types. All the beautiful men were fags. She grinned. Maybe he'd even fuck her in the bargain. It would sure beat Steve. He wouldn't know a G-spot if it ran over him. Yeah, a little money and a beautiful cock to ride to boot. She just needed a few minutes with him to look into his thoughts. Maybe she could offer him a free reading.

She was thinking about stripping the clothes off of Rallus when she heard a loud bang. She threw away her cigarette and rushed inside. Steve was chasing a terrified Michael around the room. "Come here, you little fuck. I'm going to pound your face in."

"Steve, no," she screamed. "Baby, come to Mommie."

Michael stood still now in the middle of the kitchen. "Come and get me, you prick!" he said to Steve.

"You see the way he talks to me—no respect. I'm going to teach him." Steve doubled up his fists while Sandy jumped in front of him to block his path. Steve landed her a backhand to the mouth, sending her flying.

Steve made a lunge for Michael. Michael lifted his hand. Sandy picked her head up just in time to see the glint of steel. Sandy rushed to stop him. Steve let out a yelp as he got slashed across the arm. The knife dropped to the floor.

"I don't know you anymore," Sandy whispered in horror.

"But you never did." Michael smiled.

CHAPTER SIX

Mel closed up the bar at ten o'clock. Takings weren't bad considering the weather and whatever damned curse that gypsy had put on him. He washed the glasses and felt the tension in his shoulders sit in hard lumps beneath the skin. He had run the place single-handed for two months and felt his health deteriorating. He felt older and older every single day. He'd put everything into this place. Everything to keep it open, to be the relaxing place it should be for folks to unwind.

He did a hell of an acting job when the doors were open. If only his clientele knew how poorly he slept, how dreams of running out of booze, of having no food or clean glasses haunted him . . . tortured him. He woke often, sweating and in tears, certain he could no longer cope with the pressure.

He checked the bottles. Okay for now. He'd managed to get through another night with things running smoothly. On the outside. On the inside, man, my guts ache. Cooking the meals was his favorite part, but it was a strain when he had more than a few customers needing drinks, and he had to run to the kitchen to flip steaks.

Mel made a careful notation of the cash and credit card receipts. With the phones down he couldn't verify those purchases electronically. He ran them on an old-fashioned portable machine and thankfully his credit was good enough that unless the cards were stolen, the bank would honor the charges.

He thought briefly about his ex-lover, Nick. What a cluster fuck that was. Nick, who'd gotten him a great loan and made him feel like everything was going to be okay . . . and now. Now. He gave the bartop one last swipe with a soft cloth and picked up his keys.

Mel was surprised when he heard a car stop out front. He heard footsteps and then Adrian's face appeared at the window panel by the front door.

"Hey," Mel said, feeling his smile reaching his heart.

He unlocked the door.

Adrian leaned in. "You leaving?"

"Yeah. I can get you a drink though." Mel really didn't want to get him a drink. He was exhausted, and he knew Penny would have dinner waiting, but he liked this guy and Mel was a patsy when he liked a guy.

"No, please don't go out of your way. You're probably tired. Hey, why don't we go someplace for coffee?"

Mel was so pleased he opened and closed his mouth without uttering a word.

Adrian laughed, and Mel laughed, too.

"I don't think anything's open this late around here. My sister has dinner waiting for me." Mel couldn't resist. "Why don't you come to my place? She always cooks too much, and we have coffee."

"Okay," Adrian said. "I'd like that."

Mel drove his car, Adrian following, and he parked outside the house he shared with his father and Penny.

Adrian climbed out of his car and glanced at the house. "Nice. You lived here long?"

"My dad's owned it for years. I moved in with him a couple of years ago." He hesitated as he unlocked the front door. "He's in a wheelchair, but he has his good days and bad days. Today . . . I don't know. He started off great, and then he got really weird."

He opened the door and almost fell over the empty

wheelchair in the hallway.

"Oh shit," he muttered. "Pop? Pop!"

Frantic, Mel ran down the hallway, Adrian close on his heels. He could hear laughter in the kitchen and was stunned to see his father and sister side by side at the stove.

Penny's flushed face radiated happiness.

"Who's the guy?" his father asked.

Mel gaped at him. "What?"

"Come in, come in. We cooked a feast tonight." His father rushed around the kitchen table. "Glad you brought company. Your sister the balebost, she cooks food fit for a king!"

"What's a balebost?" Adrian asked.

Penny shrugged, her head snapping in the other direction as her father dashed out the back door for firewood.

"What the hell?" Mel tottered after his father, tears in his eyes. "You're walking? But Pop . . . your spine."

Pop ran back up the few short stairs from the backyard.

"Feh! My spine, my spine. It's so much gornisht! Throw some logs on the fire and try not to make a mess."

Mel took the armful of wood wordlessly and knelt by the hearth. He fumbled with matches and newspaper, staring up at his father who was practically dancing. *What the hell is in that new medication they gave him? I haven't seen him like this in years.*

Mel felt Adrian's gaze on him and tried to smile. It was too much to hope that Pop could be so happy . . . so . . . hearty. His father slurped noisily at a spoonful of soup.

"Perfect. Come on now, let's eat."

Mel got the fire going, and when he was satisfied it was burning steadily, he joined the others at the table. Penny had gone all out with chicken and dumpling soup.

"What are these?" Adrian pointed to some cookies on a plate in the middle of the table. "He's a funny little fellow."

"That's Mr. Herxheimer," Penny said.

"Who?" Adrian asked.

Pop let loose a strange, honking laugh that made everyone else stare at him.

Penny covered the awkward moment.

"I baked them for his grieving family, for his viewing at the funeral home. I made extras as samples to take to Big Bear. There are three funeral homes and two bakeries there, plus some cafes I could try. Maybe I could get into baking celebration cookies of all kinds."

Mel beamed at her. "That's a fantastic idea, sis. You should also try that Jewish Retirement Center up on the hill."

"Oh, right! Where Mr. Herxheimer was living."

Mel nodded, breaking into a bread roll. "They must have festive occasions. You could bake kosher cookies, cakes, bread . . . all kinds of things."

"That's a great idea," Penny said.

"Bupkes!" Pop shrieked.

Adrian said, "May I try one?"

Penny nodded. "Absolutely."

He bit into a cookie.

Mel grinned. "You're eating a dead guy."

Adrian shrugged. "He's the liveliest guy I ever had in my mouth."

Mel and Penny laughed. Their father stood, an uncertain look quivering across his face.

"I hear the baby crying."

Mel started. "Baby? He still thinks that doll is the baby?"

His sister shook her head as their father went into the hallway.

"Is everything okay?" Adrian asked.

Penny sighed. "I was across the road earlier, helping the new guy, Rallus, nice guy by the way, but he has all these dolls in his house and—"

Adrian dropped his spoon with a loud clatter. "Sorry."

"And . . . and Pop showed up on foot. It was crazy! And he saw this boy doll, and he insists it's Antonio."

Adrian glanced at Mel who said, "Penny lost her entire family in a car accident. Antonio was just a baby."

He turned to his sister, whose whole demeanor had changed.

"It's okay, sis."

He moved over to put his arm around her. His sister looked suddenly deflated.

"I miss him. I wish I could believe . . . that I could take comfort in that baby doll."

"Penny, I'm so sorry." Adrian reached a hand over to Penny's and squeezed.

"Rallus let us bring the doll home. Pop's been so happy all afternoon, thinking it's Antonio."

Mel excused himself and went to look for Pop. He was sitting on the sofa, his head back, mouth agape, the baby doll swaddled in his arms.

Adrian walked up beside him. "Come on, he's okay there. He's asleep. We'll hear him if he wakes up. Come and eat. You need to eat."

He tugged at Mel's hand, leading him back to the kitchen.

Penny, clearly fighting tears, put a determined smile on her face. "Who wants pie and coffee?"

Sandy drove up to Lucinda's door and hesitated. She used to enjoy this stuff. Now she hated it. She was here at her self-appointed time of midnight because she told her gullible clients it was the witching hour. Stupid people and their stupid problems. She sighed. As weird as Mikey got during the evening, he'd become placid as a well-fed kitty after his salt bath. He was sleeping by the time she left. Steve's cut turned out to be a scratch. She'd given him some cash and sent him off drinking.

God, I hope he stays that way. Maybe this stuff we're doing . . . maybe it's bouncing back on us? Maybe I need to go home, grab Mikey, and get out of town . . . now.

Steve was back from the bars and asleep on the sofa when she left. She sometimes worried he'd run out on her when she took these assignments out of the house. It wasn't likely, considering he had no other visible means of support. The thought of his callow selfishness drove her nuts. Her fingers gripped the wheel, and she focused on breathing.

No. Lucinda's paying me five hundred dollars for this. I have two hundred hidden in the trunk. It's a good start. I'll go home and grab Mikey . . . grab whatever I can and just go.

The decision made, Sandy felt suddenly younger, energized. She almost sprinted to the purple front door of the mountain cottage and knocked.

Lucinda opened the door, and the scent of apple pie greeted Sandy.

"Thanks so much for coming." Lucinda held the folds of a purple velvet robe around her and Sandy knew she was naked underneath. Lucinda Burns was a thirty-year-old blonde who had moved to Fawnskin to start a new life. She'd fallen for the wrong guy—a married guy—and now Sandy was helping her draw the man to her with a love spell.

"I made pie and coffee," Lucinda said.

Sandy stepped into the warm cottage that seemed almost doll-size with the two of them standing in it. She was aware of the empty bookshelves that once held Lladro figurines now proudly installed in Sandy's home.

"We don't have time for that. Do you have the money?"

Lucinda's face fell. Her hands shook as she handed over the envelope stuffed full of cash.

"It's one dollar short. I'm so sorry, Sandy. I . . . I tried. I sold everything I could."

Sandy knew that Lucinda had tried. She wondered how on earth the woman had raised so much money and realized tomorrow night would be the deadline she'd given Mel to come up with his next payment. She wondered if she should stick around for that. Yes, I should wait. I've managed this long. One more day won't hurt. What if he doesn't come up with the cash?

She was aware of Lucinda's frightened gaze, aware of the skinny cat hiding under the kitchen table. She glimpsed the cans of generic cat food on the kitchen counter to her left. My God, she's scrimping on everything. She's starving her cat to pay for this. Oh, how foolish, how blind can she be?

Sandy sighed. She didn't care about the buck. She wanted this ritual over with. She almost changed her mind when Lucinda burst into grateful tears because Sandy wasn't punishing her for the lousy dollar.

Lucinda touched her shiny, blonde tresses. "I did everything except your suggestion of selling my hair. It's the one thing about me he absolutely loves."

Sandy stared at Lucinda for a moment in shock. How sad that this silly creature actually believed she was on this guy's radar.

"Let's get started," she said.

Lucinda had assembled everything Sandy had required. A red candle, a photo of her target, a red ribbon, a big cigar, a glass of water, matches, and an ashtray.

Sandy studied the photo. It was a candid snap taken of Jason King, heir to the Lakeside Funeral Home. He was married, and his wife had a new baby, but Lucinda wanted him. Sandy lit the red candle and turned to her.

"Are you ready?"

Lucinda nodded. Peeling off her robe to reveal a nude,

very trim figure, she knelt on a pillow positioned in front of the coffee table and picked up the cigar. She lit it, spluttering a little.

"You have to inhale the smoke all the way," Sandy ordered.

Lucinda looked a little frightened, but on her second puff, she did.

She held the smoke in her throat, picked up the photo and blew the smoke right on it.

"Jason King, I love you. I mean you no harm. I mean only good."

"Again," barked Sandy.

Lucinda inhaled, coughing and spluttering. Her face was green and they'd only just started.

With a determined set to her jaw, Lucinda repeated her words.

Sandy sat back on the sofa. At this rate, she'd be here for hours . . .

Adrian was a wonderful listener. Mel brought in the third pot of coffee for the night and the last of the cookies that Penny hadn't bagged up to take into stores the following day.

Mel smiled at Adrian, who lay on the hearth rug in front of the fire in the living room. Phoenix lay in her basket, drowsy from the fire. It was a happy, fuzzy picture of family life. One of the things he loved about this house was that each room had a fireplace. Adrian sat up and took the tray from Mel. The room felt great. It wasn't just the warmth, it was the scent of the logs. It was the company he was in. Mel felt the most relaxed he'd been in months. He felt so happy he hoped he wouldn't start crying like a nine-year-old girl.

"She's a wonderful woman," Adrian said, pouring milk

into his coffee. "I really hope Penny's business works out." He stirred in sugar. "So she and her husband owned a bakery, and they lost it?"

Mel hated talking about bad things when he felt this way. They'd talked about books, movies, and music, and now Adrian was bringing up difficult subjects.

"Yes, right in Big Bear. She lost it a few weeks after her husband died. They'd been scraping by, but she had no idea how badly he'd been handling the business end of things. I'm glad she's found her enthusiasm for living again."

He found himself smiling now. "It's kinda funny that making cookies for a dead guy has given her a new spark of passion. God . . . I want this for her."

Adrian stared at the fire for a moment and turned back to him. "What about you? Sounds like you've all had a tough time."

Mel nodded. "I've made some mistakes. Bad mistakes. Not just in love, but in business."

Adrian nodded. "This was the guy you mentioned . . . what's his name, Nick?"

Mel stared at him a moment. "I mentioned Nick? My God . . . I can't even remember that. I can't—"

He took a deep breath. Geez . . . when the hell did I mention Nick? I never talk about him. Did I say his name? When the hell did I mention him?

Mel put his coffee cup on the tray and stood up when he heard a noise in the next room. "That'll be my father. Excuse me a moment."

He walked toward his father's bedroom and put his ear to the door. Nothing. He felt the coolness of the wood against his cheek. Nick. He was like a tick that burrowed under his skin and hurt so bad and yet he kept burrowing, away from detection, impossible to remove.

"Mel."

He turned and found Adrian standing just a few inches from him.

"I—"

Adrian silenced whatever he was going to say with a long, deep kiss. Mel felt the tears closing in on him as strong, warm hands cupped his face.

Just as Mel got used to another man's mouth on his, just as he'd stopped wondering if his breath was okay, Adrian broke off the kiss.

"Mel," he said, his lips still grazing Mel's mouth, "please, please give me a chance. I'm not him. Whatever he did, whatever happened, I'm not Nick. I'm a good guy. Please, just . . . trust me."

"Okay," Mel said, stunned. He tried not to think about this wonderful gift. He tried not to be hurt and angry anymore. He felt . . . bewildered. How in the world had he landed a guy like this?

"Give me your tongue," Adrian whispered.

Mel thought he was hearing things, but Adrian's tongue flicked against his and Mel found himself responding. Nick had never kissed him like this. Nick couldn't kiss . . . Oh! Adrian sucked on Mel's tongue, and Mel felt the rush of heat whoosh through his entire body, ending at his swaying legs.

Rallus picked up Knox at five in the morning when Mrs. King relieved him and sent him home to sleep until noon. Rallus waited in the doorway of the closed and dark manager's office of the Golden Horseshoe Cottages, his gaze never leaving the front door of the funeral home.

Knox came out, and Rallus ran across the thin blanket of snow on the ground.

"I am so glad to see you," Knox said, and Rallus held him in his arms for a moment. He noticed a car approaching and slowing down. He was astonished to see it was Adrian, the cute guy he'd picked up a couple of days ago. Even in the dark of pre-dawn, he knew it was him.

Adrian gave him the finger, and Rallus was relieved Knox had his back to the street and couldn't see the gesture. Adrian took off with a squeal of tires and Knox turned to look.

Shit, I think he's turning around.

Rallus grabbed Knox's hand and said, "Come on, let's check out the place."

"What, are you kidding me? It's freezing."

He dragged Knox behind the first clump of cottages and heard the car slow down, but grabbed Knox's face and kissed him. The car sped off, and he saw the retreating headlights swing back again as Adrian made another pass along the street.

Rallus broke off the kiss when he was certain Adrian wasn't coming by again and noticed a pathway to the left.

"Where does that go?" he asked.

"No idea. Rallus, I'm freezing. Can't we go inside? My cabin's right here."

"No, baby, where's your sense of adventure?"

They rounded the corner and came upon a scene straight out of the Wild West. Several stores had names like Barber and Post Office but were obviously no longer in use. Immediately to their right was another establishment straight out of Gunsmoke.

"Wow, it's an old-fashioned saloon," Rallus said, his fingers squeezing Knox's frozen digits huddling for warmth against his. Snow started falling again, and Rallus pulled them under the dilapidated wooden awning. The dark, frosty windows revealed lights flickering inside and the faint sound of voices.

"Squatters," Knox said. "Let's get out of here."

"No, no, I think it's ghosts. I bet the place is haunted."

"Yeah, I bet it is, too. Let's go home."

"Don't be ridiculous. You think maybe Harold dropped in here?"

Rallus peered in the windows, and the lights disappeared inside.

"Let's go in."

"Are you crazy? Have you never seen Friday the Thirteenth or . . . or . . . any of those horror movies where crazy people go into haunted places and get carved up?"

"You're saying I'm crazy?"

"Just a little."

Rallus grinned. "Recent circumstances in my life have . . . changed me. I feel . . . I need to confront my fears head-on. I am afraid of the idea of a haunted house . . . do you suppose it really is haunted?"

He touched the door handle of the old saloon, and the voices came in hurried whispers from the other side of it. The door swung open, and the voices stopped.

"Oh, shit," Knox muttered. "It's frickin' haunted all right."

Rallus stepped forward, pulling Knox along with him.

"No," Knox said. "You might want to confront ghosts, but why do I need to go along for the ride?"

"Because," Rallus said, "I think I . . . like you."

"You're just saying that."

Rallus shook his head. "No, I'm not. Come on."

He released Knox's hand.

Knox clutched him again. "Don't let go of me."

Rallus reached into his jeans pocket and retrieved a packet of matches. He lit one. The two men stepped inside and peered into the darkness.

"We came, we saw, we peed our pants, let's go home," Knox said.

"Nuh-uh."

The match extinguished from a sudden blast of frigid air. Rallus had no idea why he really wanted to pursue this, but he did. He lit another match and was certain he could see the shimmer of ghostly figures. There was a long bar to the right. He could imagine dancing by the fireplace to the left on long, winter nights such as this.

He lit a succession of matches as snow fell heavily outside the window.

"I want to suck your cock; get it out for me," Rallus said, as Knox huddled close.

"Are you nuts?"

"Yeah. Nuts about your nuts. Get 'em out for me."

Rallus's fingers reached along the mantelpiece beside the bar. A stub of a candle sat in an old dish. He lit it. The faint flame lent an even spookier vibe to the room.

He set it on the bar top and turned to Knox who hastily unzipped his jeans. Rallus hoisted him up to it and, in spite of his qualms, he was pleased to see how willing Knox was to accommodate his wishes. Knox let out a groan as Rallus's mouth suckled at his cockhead.

"Oh, that feels good."

Rallus stood between Knox's dangling legs and made fast work of Knox's hardening cock, sucking it to the base, his lips grazing the tops of Knox's balls.

Knox tried pushing Rallus away. "You never let me suck your cock. How come I can't suck you?"

"You can. Knox unbuttoned his fly and climbed up on a bar stool. It wobbled but didn't break under his weight.

The candle flame started to ebb. He wanted to be quick. He climbed up, urging Knox to lie down on the bar, length-wise. He straddled his head, kneeling awkwardly over his lover's body, and bent down to suck Knox's cock again. It was the most amazing sixty-nine he'd ever had in his life. He felt a sharp whisper of cold against his cheek, like an icy finger stroking his skin.

He took his mouth off Knox for a moment.

"Cut it out, Harold. Get your own man."

Rallus bent toward the leaking cock at his chin once more. He didn't stop when the candle extinguished. He felt Knox humping his mouth and eased off again.

"Fuck my face," he said with a rasp, hissing with pleasure when he felt Knox lapping at his cock and balls.

Knox took possession of Rallus's mouth at the same moment Rallus toyed with Knox's ass. Both men writhed against one another, coming together as the wind shook and rattled the windows of the old saloon.

Sandy felt sick. The woman on the floor swayed with the effort of inhaling the smoke of the cigar, retching continuously. The feeling was contagious. Sandy had been here almost two hours and was ready to throw up. Lucinda heaved and wiped her mouth with the back of her hand. A black feeling, a cloud rose within Sandy. Maybe it was the thick cigar smoke in the house. Sandy thought she wouldn't be able to breathe in a second.

Lucinda trembled and sipped at the water glass, which was almost empty.

Sandy felt a strange feeling, an otherworldly pull. Oh no, the man. She heard Michael screaming in her brain and stood suddenly, the room feeling too hot, unbearable. Lucinda collapsed on the floor in convulsions.

This can't be happening.

She stared numbly at the woman, whose outstretched arm reached up to her for help. Sandy dropped the envelope of cash beside her.

Tainted money. What had she done to get this money?

"I'm leaving it; she can have it!" Sandy shouted to the

universe. But the red candle melted and wax started sliding off the candlestick. The room felt like a fire had engulfed it. She was petrified of involvement, terrified of the glimpse she'd seen of Mikey in trouble.

Sandy ran from the house in blind panic, closing the door behind her as Lucinda gasped and moaned.

"Help me!" Sandy heard her cry as she stumbled on the snow-lined walkway. She fell against the low brick fence, her knee slamming into it. She felt tears subsiding into keening shrieks.

"Mikey!"

She ran to her car and had trouble starting it. She screamed and shrieked as she tried, again and again, to turn over the engine. It started, and she floored the accelerator, going into a spin as she tried to do a U-turn. Sandy's tears stung her eyes she screamed an apology to her ancestors for every rotten thing she'd done. She could hardly see as she took the mountain road in near semi-darkness. She hit something as she turned and tried to convince herself it was a post, but she knew it was an animal. She pounded the dashboard as the car's gears started grinding in protest. All the money they'd taken from people and Steve would not let her get a new car.

Her engine burned and she heard a popping sound under the hood. The car sputtered and died in the middle of the road. When she got out and saw paws and a flattened tail under her front tire, she screamed. She left the car where it was and ran the rest of the last mile to Fawnskin.

Sandy slipped and fell in her Ugg boots several times, her left knee so badly damaged she could only drag the leg along with her as she limped into town. She tottered along North Shore Drive, which was quiet, the sound broken only by her hysterical attempts at breath. From outside her storefront, things looked okay, but she saw that the wooden gate separating the house from the business was broken.

She pushed the gate open and smelled the blood, sensed it, before she'd even made her way past Steve's body sprawled on the ground, blood seeping from him. A huge kitchen knife protruded from his back.

Sandy's mouth fell open at the sight of Mikey beside him, lying on the ground, his face pale. He was in pajamas and wore one sock. His other foot was blue from cold. She touched him, saw the blood, then . . . she screamed.

CHAPTER SEVEN

Rallus moaned, kissing Knox's come-tender cock head. A terrifying scream pierced their dark passion.

Rallus lifted his head. He scrambled off Knox, who almost fell off the bar in Rallus's haste. The two men rearranged their cocks in their pants and ran toward the direction of the screams.

"Michael," Knox said, and Rallus grabbed his hand.

They found Sandy screaming incoherently at the gate leading to her yard.

Rallus knelt beside Sandy's husband, checked his wounds, and felt a faint pulse. Michael had a pulse, too. He knelt over the young boy, checking his wounds.

"Steve's wounds are bad. He needs help I can't give. Michael might be okay."

"I'll go inside and call the police," Knox said.

"No, don't. We might be tampering with evidence."

"Payphone," Sandy sobbed. "On the corner. Only phone in town that works."

"I'll go," Knox said.

"Tell them an officer is on scene. We need an ambulance."

Knox gaped at him. "You're a cop?"

Rallus passed a hand across his brow "I was a cop. Go make the call. Be careful," Rallus shouted after him. He turned to Sandy. "What happened here?"

"I . . . I don't know. I just came home."

"Came home at this hour?"

"I was visiting a friend."

"What friend?"

"Lucinda." There was an odd expression on her face. He peered into the open back door of the house. "Was the back door open when you got here?"

"Yes."

"Have you been in?"

He took off his jacket and wrapped it around Michael's feet. Sandy was clearly in a state of shock. Nothing she said made sense.

"I felt the blackness. I felt the hate," she said.

"Sandy, I need you to turn on the light for me," he said, as he kept working on Michael. "Go inside and turn on the kitchen light."

"It's so empty and dark," she said, mumbling more non-sense.

Rallus went to the kitchen and flipped the switch.

"I knew he'd come," Sandy said, an inch behind him.

Rallus stepped forward. He saw and heard nothing.

The house appeared tidy, except for an overturned coffee table. He grabbed a couple of throw rugs from the sofa and noticed a coffee cup lying in the fireplace. It must have come off the coffee table during the struggle. He made sure not to touch anything else and went back outside.

Knox returned a few seconds later with good news.

"Help is on its way. Can you believe nine-one-one put me on hold?"

He took one of the blankets from Rallus and threw it over Steve as Rallus covered up Michael, whose eyelids opened. His unfocused eyes stayed on Knox.

"I'm so cold," he said, and Rallus assured him he'd be okay.

"Mikey!" Sandy shot forward, her voice hoarse.

"Stand back," Rallus ordered, and Sandy stood still.

They heard the wail of the ambulance and Sandy ran outside.

"You think she did this?" Knox asked him.

"I don't know. But I sure wanna keep this little guy still."

The ambulance crew arrived, and within minutes father and son were on gurneys, loaded up for the drive to Bear Valley Community Hospital.

"Where is the hospital?" Rallus asked the lone cop who showed up just as the ambulance was ready to leave.

"I'll take you there," the cop said, introducing himself as Jack Kinney. "It isn't far."

Kinney hoisted up his pants and opened the back door of his car. Sandy climbed into the ambulance and came back out.

"Mikey wants Knox to ride with him," Kinney said.

"Both of them," the paramedic in the rear shouted out.

Kinney shook his head. "You go ahead. We're right behind you."

The cop waved the ambulance away and squeezed himself behind the wheel of his vehicle, a state-issued Crown Vic.

"Shit, I gotta lose weight," he said, moving the car into drive. Over his shoulder, he glanced at Rallus and Knox sitting in the backseat.

"Any idea what went down?"

The two men told him what they knew, which wasn't much. They arrived at the hospital, which wasn't an impressive-looking facility, but the cop assured them they'd handled domestic violence disputes before.

"You think she did it?" Rallus asked.

The cop eased himself out from the wheel. "Ozzie and Harriet, they are not. We've had thirty calls out to their place in the last six months."

He shook his legs, one after the other. Rallus realized the cop didn't want to go inside straight away. He stood under the one parking spotlight outside the entrance. He sucked on his lower lip a moment, his feet apart, huge belly jutting forward. He reminded Rallus of Fred Mertz in I Love Lucy.

"How well you know this gal, his mom?" Kinney asked.

"I don't know her at all," Knox said, "except her kid disappeared day before yesterday and we found him."

Kinney nodded. "We've had a few complaints. Folks say she's a gypsy. You know anything about that?"

"She is," Rallus said. "A very aggressive one."

He was aware of Knox's astonished gaze. "I've heard her strong-arming people. We had a few like her up where I'm from."

"And where is that?" Kinney asked.

Rallus hesitated. "Monterey."

Kinney nodded. "'Spose I'd better go in."

Inside the hospital, Sandy paced the waiting room. The doctor came out and beckoned her through a set of swinging doors.

Knox and Rallus took seats as Kinney ambled over to the admissions desk where the night nurse greeted him. The place was quiet.

"You didn't tell me you were a cop."

Rallus shrugged. "You didn't ask."

"Wise ass," Knox said. "Cops are kinda sexy."

Rallus raised a brow in his direction. "All cops?"

"No. Just you."

Rallus leaned over and kissed him.

"Were you a cop in Alaska?"

"No. Just Monterey."

"And you retired?"

"Took a leave of absence."

"Why?"

"I needed some time off."

Sandy came out, her eyes brimming with tears. She held a

cotton ball to her arm.

She must have given blood. Rallus watched the cop talking to her, then returned his attention to Knox.

"I'm a good cop. I just needed personal time."

Neither man said anything for a minute.

Sandy stomped over to them. "That man makes me so mad. He makes me feel like I did it. He wanted to know where I was tonight . . . my client's name and everything."

"Any news?" Knox asked her.

"They're working on Steve . . . he has seven stab wounds . . . they don't think there's much hope."

She didn't look devastated at that news, Rallus noticed.

"They don't think he'll make it if they airlift him to LA, but they're trying surgery. Mikey has one stab wound. It's quite deep, but they tell me he should be okay. They want to give him a transfusion. I—"

Her face went slack.

Rallus put his hand on her arm. "I am sure this is a terrible shock."

"It's the blood," she said. "Oh, my God. I never thought about it."

"What about it?"

Sandy leaned forward and put her head between her legs.

"Can I get you something? Anything?" Rallus asked as Sandy howled into her bare hands.

"Is there anyone I can call for you?" Rallus asked. "Any family member? A friend?"

"No," she said, bitterness seeping into her voice. "We have nobody. I just want my baby to be okay."

Rallus wasn't sure what to make of this woman. She clearly loved her son, also equally seemed to despise her husband. Enough to stab him and the little kid? In his years as a cop, he'd heard the bizarre reasons people had for hurting the ones they loved. He wouldn't put it past Sandy to have done this for attention . . . or some other weird motive.

The cop paced, keeping his distance. Rallus fancied that Kinney felt comfortable knowing Rallus was with the wife. At one point, he looked up and saw the doctor talking to the cop, and he knew, just knew that it was bad news.

The doctor came over to them, his gaze on Sandy, who looked up and clutched Rallus.

"Oh, God . . . please tell me he's okay."

"I'm sorry, but your husband passed just a few minutes ago."

A nurse came out with a quick glance at Sandy and handed the doctor a piece of paper. Sandy barely had time to absorb the first piece of news before he delivered the second blow.

"We have another problem. Michael lost a lot of blood—"

"Yes, yes," she said, her body starting to shake. "I already said I was willing to give him blood. Anything he needs. Please . . ."

"Well, that's just it. We just checked your sample against his blood type and against your husband's. There's no match."

"Oh, my God, no."

"He has a very unusual blood type I've never seen before. It's so rare I had to email my colleagues in Los Angeles to ask their advice. Michael is AB Negative, which is a very rare blood type. There's certainly nothing on hand we can give him."

Sandy fell on the floor, aware of people staring at her as she let out a keening wail.

The doctor talked over her, reading from the page in his hand.

"Michael also has a specific blood response, Duffy Negative, which we normally see in African American families. Without an immediate infusion of it, he'll deteriorate rapidly. I can't give him type O—his body won't tolerate it. In fact, with his blood type, it could prove fatal. I want to airlift him to Los Angeles, but Mrs. DiNozza, you need to tell me now. Whose child is he?"

Shit. Sandy bit her bottom lip. How could she tell them the truth? They'd take her baby away if they knew how Mikey had come to be hers.

She glanced around the room trying to come up with a plausible story. If she could just buy herself some time, perhaps Mikey would be released, and she could take him away from Fawnskin before the truth came out.

"Steve and I were unable to have children. So when a young girl came to us and offered to let us raise Mikey, we were overjoyed."

The policeman who had answered the call at her house stepped forward. "What's this woman's name?"

Sandy swallowed around the lie. "It was so long ago, but I think her name was Janice, Janet, Jannette, something like that."

The cop wrote something on his small pad of paper. "Last name?"

Sandy shook her head. "I don't know. She lived in the apartment building across the street from the mobile-home park where we lived. She said she thought she could raise Mikey on her own, but all her girlfriends had deserted her, and she was too young to be saddled with a toddler."

Rallus snorted. "Right. And where is this make-believe city where people just hand over their children?"

"We were living in Bakersfield at the time. I'm telling you the truth."

"I'll handle this," the cop told Rallus. "Did you legally adopt Michael?"

Sandy shook her head and stared at the floor. "We couldn't afford it. We gave the girl money for a bus ticket and have been raising Mikey ever since."

"She's lying!" Rallus murmured.

Knox reached out and put a hand on his lover's arm. The last thing they needed was for Rallus to get hauled off to jail for interfering in an investigation.

With a narrowed gaze, Sandy stared at Rallus. "Can't we talk about this without him around?"

The doctor led Sandy and the policeman to a small consultation room. Knox leaned against Rallus. "You really think she's lying?"

Rallus wrapped an arm around Knox. "Did you notice her eyes before she started telling that elaborate story? She's scared. And not just about how she really laid her hands on Mikey."

Knox listened as Rallus practically interrogated the policeman on the way back to town. Obviously, he wasn't satisfied with the way things had gone. Knox was sure there was going to be a fight. "I'm thinking that you're calling me an incompetent," Kinney muttered from the front seat of the cruiser.

Rallus didn't answer, which spoke volumes.

"In all due respect, I'm the law in this town, and you're just some . . ."

"I think we should all calm down," Knox said suddenly.

"I can't believe you just let her go. What else did she say? Did she tell you how she got that boy? He's not hers. I wouldn't be surprised if she kidnapped him or bought him on the black market."

"You don't know that. We haven't got any proof. Anyway, I can't discuss this with you. You're not on the job anymore."

"You need to find out how she makes her money. That husband of hers doesn't work, and yet they seem to live fine."

"I'll look into it."

"When? Eventually, that boy is going to get out of that hospital, and she's going to find him and run with him."

"Okay, you're speculating."

"Isn't that what good investigators do?"

"You miss your job," Kinney said as he pulled into town and parked on Main Street.

"Don't patronize me. This has nothing to do with missing my fucking job. This is about that boy."

"Calm down," Knox placed a hand on his arm.

The cop got out of the car, and Rallus shook off Knox's hand. Knox sighed and got out of the backseat with Rallus.

Rallus began to walk, trudging straight ahead in the snow. Knox chased after him. "Rallus. Can you tell me what's going on with you?"

"I hate incompetence," he said between clenched teeth, but he didn't slow his pace.

"Why didn't you tell me you were . . ."

He paused, turned around. There was the faintest dusting of snow on his head. "Do you need to know everything about me? You're fucking me, isn't that enough?"

Knox's face fell.

Rallus muttered something and threw up his hands. "I'm sorry. You don't understand. It's not your fault. Sometimes time is . . . time is precious, minutes, even seconds tick away, and it changes everything."

Knox sighed. "What do you think happened?"

"I don't know. It's goddamn strange. If it's a spirit, it's one hell of a one."

"Do you think Herxheimer wanted to kill Steve for some

reason and used Michael to do it?"

"It's possible. I feel like I'm in an episode of The X-Files." Knox laughed.

"When are you back on dead watch?" Rallus placed an arm around him.

"I got an hour."

Rallus grinned. "That should be long enough. Come on."

"No more creepy places."

"Wouldn't dream of it," he said.

There was so much he wanted to know, so many questions, but when Rallus's lips touched his, and he felt his erection against his hip, all sane thoughts deserted him. "God," he moaned, tearing at his shirt, wanting nothing except to feel his hard, naked body against him, "get those pants off."

Rallus laughed, helping Knox take off his pants and allowing him to push him down on the bed, popping the buttons on his shirt and planting his lips on his bare flesh. Oh God, I think I love this man. I can't get enough.

Rallus moaned as Knox licked around each nipple and massaged his balls in his hand. He moved up and straddled Rallus's hips, moving his hips so that Rallus's hard cock brushed between his legs a few times. "Want to fuck me?"

"Oh yeah," Rallus said, licking his lips.

"Not yet," Knox whispered, leaning down and kissing his eyelids, his mouth, his throat. "How badly you want my ass?"

"Bad enough to just take it." He groaned.

"Then do it, stud. Put your cock where my ass is."

Rallus laughed. "Joker. Spread your thighs and open up. I'm going to fuck you deep and hard. Ride me."

"Oh yeah." He gasped as Rallus began to open his ass, moving his finger inside him up to the knuckle. Knox let his head go back, spreading his thighs wider to give him access. Rallus inserted another finger, slowly going in and out, touching every nerve inside the tunnel. Knox reached up and pinched his own nipples hard, moving his fingertips over each nub as he felt the head of Rallus's cock stab inside him. "Oh God, um . . . yeah." He was so open and suddenly felt so hot.

"Um, you like that?" Rallus's cock moved in deeper as he lifted his hips higher and Knox sank onto the cum-coated rod.

"Fuck me," he cried out. "Yeah, oh yeah, fuck me," he urged.

Rallus's cock sank deeper still, then pulled out and snaked all the way in again, working up to a faster pace as time ticked away. The fucking took Knox away. He lost all sense of time, all sense of reality, and when he came, he screamed his release like an elated warrior who'd just had his first victory in battle.

He slid down beside Rallus when it was over, holding on-to him for dear life, breathing in his skin. "Rallus."

"It would be good if you didn't fall in love with me, Knox."

"Too late for that."

He fell silent.

"So, why didn't you quit?"

"Quit what?"

"Being a cop?"

"I didn't quit."

"But . . ."

"Let's drop it. I'm happy right now. I don't want to think."

Ten minutes later, Knox was in Rallus's shower. Don't fall in love with me.

Those words haunted him as he dressed and prepared to head back to work.

Rallus walked with him as they headed toward the funeral home. "It's going to a long night. You're going to be tired."

"What with everything that's happened, I doubt I could sleep. I'm running on adrenaline. I wonder how Michael is."

"I'll call and find out."

They were standing outside Mrs. King's now, the snow softly falling. "Why did you say that?"

"Say what?"

"'Don't fall in love with me.'"

"Did I say that?"

"Don't be coy."

He smiled.

"You're not going to answer, are you?"

"I have my reasons."

"A man of mystery."

"Which is part of my appeal, right?" He grinned.

"Among other things." Knox let his gaze move down over him.

Rallus laughed out loud. "You better go in. She's peering out the window."

"Good, then let's give her something to look at." Knox leaned forward and kissed Rallus passionately on the mouth. When he let him go, Rallus winked at him.

"That should do it. See you later?"

"Um. You bet your sweet everything."

Rallus laughed as he walked away.

Mrs. King came to greet him at the door. "He is a handsome man," she said as if that summed it all up.

"All over," he muttered and laughed to himself. "I'm sorry," he said when she didn't share his joke. He sobered. "I suppose you've heard."

"Some."

"Michael stabbed his father, or stepfather really, and he's dead. Do you think it was Harold?"

"I presume," she said, putting her fingers together. "But why? I can't see that selfish man doing it for the boy. And Michael, how is he?"

"Bad. He needs blood, and he has a rare blood type."

"I'm sorry to hear that."

"I think Harold has moved on now. He's not here, is he?"

She shook her head. "I can't get the candles to stay lit."

"Then where?"

"I don't know."

"You think he attached himself to someone else?"

"Possibly, they can do that. Hungry?"

"I'm always hungry."

"I'll get you something, and then you can go to work."

He reached and squeezed her hand. "Thanks for not blaming me."

"Oi! What 'cha gonna do? A man's gotta pee."

A few hours before, Adrian had watched Rallus as he got out of the cop car. He was with his boyfriend again, and he looked pissed about something. He watched as the boyfriend ran after him down the street. Where the hell were they going?

A lot of the residents had been out in pajamas and thick coats, and he already knew a murder had taken place. He'd spoken to enough people to know there were two people attacked. A small kid survived. He thought about approaching the cops. He wanted to pick up new business but he had his hands full with the Mel Gower investigation. He pondered his next move now as he watched the waking dawn break across the sky in shades of lavender and gray. It was as if it, too, struggled with bad news.

He badly wanted to step right in front of the guy who'd given him the most incredible sex of his life and then abandoned him. He wanted to confront him. Who the hell was the boyfriend? Why did Rallus cheat on him if he was so hot? Adrian was about to start his engine when he realized Rallus had seen him. It was like Robo Cop had spotted him. Crud on a bagel. A glance, a look away, recognition processing, and the head swiveling back again. The sharp expression was no welcome mat.

Shit! Rallus walked toward him, a determination to his confident gait. He rapped on the passenger window; Adrian's fingers still gripping the wheel. He knew his mouth hung open and realized he must look like a gulping guppy, but he popped the lock and Rallus slid in beside him.

God . . . the nearness of him.

"What are you doing here?" Rallus asked.

"I'm working a case in town . . . I heard what happened."

"You're a private investigator, right?"

Adrian felt his stomach muscles flip-flop.

"How did —"

"You told me, first night we met. You don't remember?"

Adrian shook his head in disbelief. "I sure don't remember that."

Rallus shifted in the seat, rubbing his hands together. "You gave me some shit about decorating or drawing or something —"

"Architect," Adrian mumbled.

"Yeah, right. But I saw the way you were eye-huntin' on that poor bar owner. What do you have him pegged for, anyway?"

Shit. "You're a cop." Adrian slapped his forehead. "I shoulda known."

"Retired."

"Doesn't look like it."

Rallus shrugged. "You can't take the cop outta the guy sometimes . . ."

Adrian was nervous. "You think Mel Gower figured I was on his tail?"

Rallus stared at him a moment. "Not that night. He seemed stressed out. You know, his family's having a bad time."

"Yeah." Adrian's thumbnail rubbed against a nick in the steering wheel leather.

"What's he supposed to have done?"

Adrian felt his whole case blowing to shit in a hand-woven Fawnskin basket.

"Bank job. A lot of money. His lover's in jail waiting for arraignment, but says Mel was in on it."

Rallus scoffed. "And you believe that? Have you seen the house he's living in? Seen the inside of that bar?"

Adrian lifted his hands. "I know, I know. It's not making sense to me either, but I got a job to do, and I'm getting paid."

Rallus nodded. "They're nice people. Old man's a little weird, but Mel and his sister . . . they're okay. Hey, you hear anything about the chick Sandy, whose kid got stabbed? "

Adrian hesitated. If he offered up information, maybe Rallus wouldn't blow his cover.

"I'm not interested in perverting the course of justice," Rallus said.

Shit, he's a mind reader.

"I'll let you spin your wheels with Mel . . . it just seems a strange coincidence you come here, and this happens."

Adrian gaped. "You think I stabbed these people?"

"No, you idiot. But I think you know something about her. I saw you outside her door a couple of days ago."

Adrian started. "You saw —"

"What do you know about her?"

"Okay, I'll bite. She's extorted a lot of money from a lot of folks —"

"Mel included?"

"Mel included."

"She went after his sister," Rallus said. "I overheard them in the store."

Adrian absorbed this. "She and her husband . . . the guy who was murdered . . . well, they had a lot of action in Riverside County and criminal complaints in LA County."

"Interesting. Under what names?"

Adrian grinned. "She works as Sandy here. I made an appointment but never saw her."

"You made an appointment? Why?" Rallus asked.

"A friend suggested it."

"But you heard these things about her and still went to see her? "

Adrian nodded. "I wasn't sure it was the same woman . . . but it is. Look, I was working on something . . . not related to this, okay?"

He reached across the seat, felt Rallus recoil, and it gutted him. He snapped open the glove compartment and withdrew a slip of paper. He passed it to Rallus, who flipped the switch on the roof for light and unfolded the page.

"Crap. How many aliases these people got?"

Adrian glanced at the police report. He wasn't going to tell Rallus everything.

"A lot."

"This is gonna make it harder to track down the kid's DNA," Rallus said.

Adrian was confused. "Kid?"

"Sandy's kid, Michael. He isn't theirs."

Adrian shrugged. "Doesn't surprise me. She steals everything, allegedly. They left town awful fast a few months ago."

Rallus tapped the page. "Idyllwild."

"Right. No reports since, but I was pretty sure she was the

same woman from another investigation my company is working on in Big Bear. Same M.O. I think . . . well, most of the reports I read, I was surprised she hadn't done serious time, but she was arrested and always got bailed out. She's got friends in high places or something. You know, you might wanna talk to Riverside County Sheriff. There's an extensive file on 'em there. They bounced around a bit, but the last five years they were there. Maybe there's a missing kid who fits the description."

"Hey, I appreciate the tip."

"No problem."

"No, I mean it. You didn't see the crime scene. Man, I've been a cop a long time, and it fucking blew me away. Mind if I take this?"

Adrian shook his head. "No can do. I pulled strings."

"All right. Mind if I make some notes?"

"Go crazy."

Rallus rolled his eyes and withdrew a pen and small notebook from his back pocket. He lifted his ass as he did this and his crotch jutted into the air. Adrian winced. Man, how can I still want him?

He waited, the sound of Rallus's pen scribbling across the notebook a comforting sound. This small moment was unexpected and welcome. He wanted to mention the other night. He wanted to say something . . .

"You're very thorough," Rallus said, handing him back the report.

"Thanks."

"I mean it. You know, if you're looking at her because she extorted money from your guy—how do you know about that, by the way?"

"Bank account."

"Then you don't see any huge deposit?"

"Nope. But a lot of withdrawals and Mel told a friend of

his who told me that she was extorting him. The amounts tallied with the withdrawals."

"This friend being . . ."

"His former lover."

Rallus stared at him. "So they talked on the phone. The former lover's in jail, and the call was recorded? Or . . . did he tell you?"

Shit. This guy fucking knows everything. "Yeah."

"I think you're a thorough guy, like I said. Thanks for the info on Sandy or Sugar or Estrella . . . or whoever the fuck she really is."

"Not a problem."

Rallus reached over and touched his hand. "You know . . . what happened the other night . . . I'm . . ." He blew out a breath and silence wrestled between them with unspoken words warring for a voice. "I never meant to lead you on. I never . . . I've met someone, and he's a cool guy, and I'm gonna pursue it. I like him, Adrian. I hope it's gonna be okay with you because I don't want any problems. I got enough."

Adrian swallowed. "That night, why did you blindfold me?"

"You liked it, didn't you?"

"Yeah, I liked it, but why? You didn't want me to know where you lived or what? I haven't figured that out yet."

Rallus shrugged. "There's not much sense in memorizing the face of the dead."

Adrian shook his head. "What?"

Rallus didn't answer. He just got out of the car.

"Why him, that stranger who just blew into town, and not me?" he called out as Rallus closed the car door.

Shit! Rallus stared at him from the sidewalk. He lifted his shoulders. "Really, you're the lucky one, Adrian, although you don't realize it now."

"How so?"

"You'll get off in the end without feeling the pain." He mouthed sorry and walked back to the crime scene.

Yeah, pal, I'm sorry, too. But pain would have been well worth it for you . . . whatever pain he was going on about.

"His name is Nick." Penny fought sleep to hunt for the rest of his name.

Rallus patted her hand. "It's important, Penny."

She nodded. "Let me make coffee." She got up from the breakfast table and moved to the coffeemaker on the counter. Five-forty in the morning and barely any sleep. She didn't want to wake Mel to ask him. It was the first night she'd seen him happy in a long, long time.

She spooned coffee into the French press and turned on the electric kettle. When she turned around, Rallus's grave eyes were on her.

"Brash," she said. "Wow, that's it. His name is Nick Brash."

"Great, thanks."

She opened the cupboard and withdrew her best Noritake coffee cups.

"You want some homemade lemon muffins?" she asked.

Rallus's grin told her everything.

"I'll have 'em on the table in fifteen minutes. But first, you mind bringing me two lemons from the box right out the back door?"

"Please don't go to any trouble."

"It's no trouble. Pop loves them, and all of a sudden he wants to eat. Usually, he doesn't. His meds help with the Alzheimers but mess with his digestive system."

Rallus opened the back door, and Penny watched him hunt through her old icebox for the lemons. Beyond the trees in her yard, she saw whispers of pink in the sky. Lord, it was beautiful here.

She measured flour, sugar, unsalted butter, lemon rind, lemon juice, a healthy dollop of lemon curd, some chopped, candied ginger and lemon peel, and cracked an egg.

"I could eat it like that," Rallus, said, closing the back door and leaning against the counter.

"That's what Mel always says."

"You're a fantastic cook."

She blushed. "Thanks."

Aware of his stare as she prepared the paper cups in the muffin tray, she sighed.

"Go ahead and ask. I'd rather you asked me. Mel's... Mel's stress level is past the red zone and heading to the emergency room.

"Can you tell me what you know about the robbery?"

She banged the pan against the counter top. "It started with cards."

"Cards?"

"A bunch of guys played poker. Gay guys. You might not know this, but being gay isn't exactly a . . . cause for celebration in Fawnskin. I'm not saying there aren't gay men here. There are . . . but most of them . . . well, they're weekend warriors. They live in LA and come here for weekends. They ski, they snowboard, they shop for antiques. It's their little bit of mountain paradise. For single gay guys living here, it's tough."

The kettle clicked off, and she filled the press to the silver line and put the lid on. She spooned her cake mix into the last empty paper cup and slid the pan in the oven.

"So, Mel, who was anxious to buy the bar, was the manager and the guy who owned it let Mel do what he wanted. The owner was in LA and didn't really care what Mel did as long as the bills were paid. So, Mel got this idea that on weekends, they could have gay poker nights. It was every

Sunday and, believe it or not, it was a huge hit. Mel really filled a hole in the social calendar. He had food, brought in, wines from different countries, music, and . . . poker. It was fun. No big pots. It was just fun."

She heard her own voice rising.

"What happened?" Rallus asked her.

"Cream? Sugar?"

"Sugar, thanks."

"What usually happens? A few drinks too many and people start pairing off, people develop attractions. He met Nick Brash, who worked at the bank in Riverside that gave Mel his business loan. I think Nick liked Mel to begin with and rushed the loan through. Of course, Mel took a mortgage on the house, too, when he realized how much work the bar needed. The loan he got from the bank had a huge interest rate. It wasn't supposed to be so high, and then Nick started drinking."

She paused. "I didn't like him when I met him. I warned Mel, but he was lonely up here and working all the time." She pushed the plunger down; a few drops of hot liquid rushed over the spout and burned her hand.

Rallus put a dishcloth over her palm. "You okay?"

"Yeah, thanks. That was weird."

"So, what happened?"

"Well, the first thing I remember is some money went missing at the bank on a day Nick was working as a teller, and the bank blamed him. They were short, like seventeen thousand dollars short. A lot of money. He denied it and became very upset. He hired a lawyer, and they took him off being a teller. A couple of weeks later there was a huge robbery and two million dollars was stolen."

She poured the coffee, checked the time. Fifteen minutes and the muffins would be ready.

Rallus moved to the table with her. She felt his gaze on

her face, willing her to share her knowledge.

"The bank manager woke up one morning to find two men standing by his bed. His wife screamed, and they knocked her out with the butt of the gun."

"Wow, I didn't know that part."

She nodded, stirring her coffee. "They made him drive to the bank, he opened the safe, he did all the right things, pressed all the alarm codes, but the police were slow. He said he knew one of the guys was Nick Brash."

"How were they dressed?"

"Ski masks, black clothing."

"How did he know it was Nick?"

She hesitated. "Nick's got a very distinctive accent. He's from Ireland, and it's a heavy accent. He didn't say anything. The other guy did all the talking until the cops arrived. Nick swore and told the other guy to hurry and, well, they fired a shot at the bank manager and missed. He went down anyway, pretending he'd been hit. Nick told the other guy, 'Shoot him again.' That's when the bank manager, Frank Cantor, heard his voice and knew it was Nick." She sipped her coffee. She hadn't witnessed the crime, but in her mind, the scene had played over and over once her brother became implicated.

"They ran out. The cops caught Nick a couple of hours later, but he didn't have the money. He tried to deny it was him, but once he realized the gig was up, he claimed my brother was the other guy."

"And was it?"

"Of course not. My brother's guilty of being a dumb ass, but he's no crook."

"You want a little more coffee?"

"Sure, if you wouldn't mind."

"So who do you think the other guy was?" Rallus asked.

Penny bit her lip.

"It's important, Penny."

"I have no proof. It's just what I . . . think. What Mel and I both think."

"Who?" he asked.

"Steve. The guy who just got murdered."

CHAPTER EIGHT

Kinney leaned against the rickety old fence outside Sandy's house and scratched his chin. He'd just had his authority on the case usurped by the Riverside County police department, and he was in a foul mood.

"I remember reading something about it . . . don't remember reading about Mel being mixed up in any bank robbery, though."

"He's not mixed up in it." Rallus began to panic. Kinney was both stupid and full of pride. A dangerous combination. The last thing Rallus needed was for Mel to have his name blasted around a small town as a bank robber.

"What I tried to say was that Mel used to have poker nights at his bar. Sunday nights, I believe. One of the guys got arrested for bank robbery in Riverside, and he's in jail."

"Well, round these parts, what happens in Riverside, stays in Riverside."

Kinney seemed to be enjoying his little joke, but Rallus was pissed. This was big news. Penny didn't know much more than what she'd told Rallus. When she tried to awaken her brother to ask him to talk to Rallus, he was gone.

"Phone lines are up one minute, down the next," she'd said, "but this is his cell phone number."

"What we got here, a murder and an attempted murder is bigger than a bank heist," Kinney said, eyeing the crime scene investigators swarming the house.

A news crew was out front, and Rallus could tell Kinney was sucking in his gut in case they were filming him.

"I think they're connected," Rallus told him, but Kinney was giving a little wave to the film crew, so Rallus blew past him to the back door of the house.

A uniformed officer stopped him. "Sir, you can't come in."

"It's okay, Sid," another voice said. Rallus smiled at the newly assigned lead detective to whom he'd already spoken. He and Detective Fisk had already chatted and Fisk, though appreciative of Rallus's big-town experience had made it known in a very polite way that he didn't need Rallus's help.

"I have some information you might need," Rallus said.

"Go on, I'm listening." Fisk, a slim, balding man in his fifties, was a lot more on the ball than Kinney, but then Fisk was out of Riverside and had to be tough and smart to work in a big city with some major crime.

Rallus ran through what he knew about Sandy.

"We have the little boy's blood going through the system now. The FBI is involved. We have a field team at the hospital now."

"Any news on Mikey?" Rallus asked.

"He's critical. The Feds have been fantastic." He held up an iPhone. "They got the local TV networks involved, and Michael's picture is all over the country. We're checking DNA of course, and we've got a bunch of missing children's advocates spreading the word online." He paused. "We're also trying to find blood to match his. Apparently, many African Americans and some native Americans share his strain. A hospital in Taos, New Mexico has some."

"That's fantastic news."

Fisk nodded, staring into the house. "We found some really disturbing things. I'd value your opinion. I—" He seemed emotional now, not unusual in a violent case involving a small child. Sid, we got an extra set of paper booties?"

The sullen cop handed them over, and Rallus hopped

from one foot to the other slipping them over his shoes. He took a pair of fresh latex gloves from Sid and thanked him. He'd already told Fisk he'd been inside the house when first discovering the crime, but now as he followed the detective inside, he felt the creepiness of the place envelop him.

They walked into the bedroom, where Rallus was surprised to see the place stacked high with boxes and bags and dozens of racks of clothing.

"Tell me what you make of this," Fisk said over his shoulder as a crime scene investigator came out of what looked like a walk-in closet.

"I'm Catholic," he said. "I can't touch this stuff."

Fisk sighed. "Okay, Donnie. Leave it to me."

Three guys crowded around the entrance, one of them filming it. They stood back as Fisk arrived and Rallus balked at the initial, gory impact. A dead animal lay on the floor, pushed up against the far wall.

"Is that a kid?" he asked, realizing it was indeed a baby goat. Its throat had been cut, its head smashed. Burned-down red and black candles surrounded it. Rallus couldn't bear to see the tiny cloven feet lying neatly at the other end of the dead kid's body.

Rallus took in the rest of the room. My God. There were religious pictures placed high on the wall and on what would have been the top shelf for purses, stood dozens and dozens of photos, candid photos pasted on boards. Rallus studied the images and recognized a few of the locals.

"What do you make of this?" Fisk gestured at a man's shoe into which a glass of liquid had been stuffed. Perched over the liquid but not quite touching it was a very smelly egg out of which protruded long, rusty nails, which held the egg over the liquid.

Rallus bent and sniffed.

"Urine." He knelt in front of it. He realized there was a

cutout photo inserted under the shoelaces.

"This photo is of Mel Gower. I just learned Sandy was extorting him for money."

Fisk snorted. "He's not the only one."

Rallus straightened, and Fisk pointed to the photos.

"She had something on everyone in town it looks like. We found all kinds of surveillance gear, very high tech stuff in the second bedroom."

Rallus was stunned to see a photo of himself and one of Knox. Protectiveness welled in him. As he studied each ghastly shrine in the room, he realized each offering corresponded with an image on the shelf.

"The only ones that don't have offerings are me and Knox and this lady. Any idea who she is?"

"Geez," Fisk said. "Doesn't look like Sandy's been doing love spells. This stuff is . . ."

"Full of hate."

"Who's this woman?" Rallus asked, indicating the pretty blonde again.

Fisk picked up the photo. "No idea." He turned it around. "Lucinda Burns."

"Sandy told me she'd been with somebody called Lucinda when this happened," he said.

"Good. I'll check that out."

Rallus turned back to the macabre gallery of horrors.

"I think she's systematically worked each of these people. There's red candle wax at the bottom of this photo," Rallus said. "Some have red, some have black. There's nothing on mine or Knox's." Thank God. "I bet Sandy started working on her last night."

He pointed to a photo a few inches away. "Who's that?"

Fisk picked it up, his gloved fingers squeaking a little. "Nick Brash."

Rallus nodded. "Interesting."

"That's the guy you just told me about," Fisk said.

"Yep, and I'm worried now."

"Worried? About Brash?"

"Yup."

"Why?"

"See the offering for him?" He pointed again. A voodoo doll hidden in the corner had the same photo pasted on the face. The voodoo doll had a rope around its neck.

"I'm betting this guy's about to have a very nasty accident inside his jail cell."

Fisk and the others looked at each other and, within seconds, Rallus found himself escorted out of the house. He soon found himself on the same stretch of sidewalk as Kinney.

"You got booted, too, huh?"

"Yeah." Rallus felt defeated. Defeated and helpless. He knew it all tied in together, but without his gun and badge, he was useless. He couldn't make anyone listen to him.

Knox yawned and stretched4. Tiredness . . . even exhaustion didn't begin to describe how he felt. He sipped the hot green tea in his hands at the kitchen table as Penny pressed a turkey sandwich into his hands.

"It's kosher," she said, as if on automatic pilot.

"Thanks, but I'm not Jewish," he mumbled, "just very, very hungry." He bit into the soft bread. Man, it was good. He chewed steadily, trying to keep the vision of Steve and Mikey's bodies out of his mind. He had to eat. He had to work. His eyes started to tear. Man, he missed Curtis so much. He wanted to drive back and get him, but he still hadn't been paid. He lost track of how much Mrs. King owed him, and his gas tank was empty.

She was so stressed out, he hated to ask her for the money, but he needed it.

"Knox," Mrs. King said, poking her head into the room.

"You need me to sit?" he asked.

"No, hon. Put on the TV. Somebody said they just arrested Sandy."

Knox and Penny looked at each other in shock.

Mrs. King yelled, "Hurry. We have a viewing in twenty minutes. I want to get the lowdown. The remote's on top of the microwave."

Penny grabbed it, and for the first time, Knox realized there was a TV in the corner of the kitchen. Penny found the report and they watched enthralled as the newsflash said Sandy had been arrested at Cedars Sinai Hospital. She'd been trying to escape and had been trapped in a stairwell.

They watched her being led away in handcuffs, her head hanging low.

"My God!" Mrs. King's hand flew to her mouth. "They're treating her like a criminal."

The solemn-faced brunette on TV stood outside Cedars Sinai. "Sources say that Sandy DiNozza had a number of aliases . . ."

"Knox."

He turned his head and was so pleased to see Rallus that nothing else in the world existed. He saw the same . . . relief in Rallus's eyes. The sheer pleasure of being together again was a feeling Knox hadn't experienced in a long time. He felt a momentary giddiness he swore was swimming right back at him.

"Go get some rest," Mrs. King told him, and he almost laughed at the gleeful smile on Rallus's face.

"Mrs. King—"

"Not another word," she said, touching his cheek. "I want you to get some rest. You take the whole day and come back tomorrow."

His heart sank. "Tomorrow?"

"Yes. Come in at nine. We have a service at eleven, and I could use your help. Oh, say, I haven't paid you yet, have I?"

"No."

She beckoned him, and he and Rallus followed her to the office. Knox was ecstatic when she rummaged through a drawer, took out her checkbook and wrote out a check for five hundred dollars.

"I'm giving you a fifty dollar tip," she said.

He thought he might faint. "A tip?"

"You've been wonderful." She grabbed him into a hug. "You're like another son to me."

They walked into the chilly foyer, and the front door swung open.

Jason King stood there, weeping.

"Oh, my God, what's happened?" Mrs. King asked. "Nothing's wrong with the baby? Please tell me he's okay."

"He's fine." One hand moved to his face, the other gripped the doorframe. "They just found Lucinda. She's — she's dead, Mom."

Mrs. King's face turned pale. "You foolish —"

She turned to Knox and Rallus. "Don't mind us. Lucinda's an old family friend." Her glance at her son was reproachful. "A crazy lady. You two run along. See you in the morning."

"Thanks." Knox's voice was soft when he spoke to Jason. "I'm very sorry for your loss."

"I'm not," Mrs. King said, her voice fake-bright. "Business is booming for us!"

Outside, once they got past the hysterical Jason, Knox almost exploded. "Can you believe her?"

Rallus was quiet.

Knox was anxious now. "Was it something I said?"

"No, baby. I . . ."

"Tell me."

Rallus shrugged. "I found out Sandy was with a girl called Lucinda when Mikey was being attacked."

"Wow. That's huge. Don't you think it's weird people are dropping like flies around here?"

The front door flew open again as they walked down the path and Mrs. King, looking a lot happier than she should, marched down the path toward them.

"Sweetie, so glad I found you. Um . . . it's a little embarrassing. I know I said you could stay at the cabin, but with all the funerals we're having, we need to rent it out . . . unless you're thinking of . . . um . . . paying for it yourself?"

The sweet moment had been too good to last. He sucked in a breath. "How much—"

"He won't need it," Rallus said. "He's going to stay with me."

She looked from one to the other, intense curiosity in her gaze. "Really?"

Knox stared at Rallus, who chuckled.

"Yes, he is. We'll go over and get his things out right now."

Some people were parking out front and by the grief etched into their features, Knox suspected Mrs. King had some new business on her hands.

"Wonderful," she said, her gaze already on her fresh quarry.

Adrian debated his next move. He felt a ridiculous bubble of hope. Rallus didn't think Mel was guilty. Hell, he didn't think Mel was guilty. He'd planned to seduce the guy to get him to fess up. He wondered now if he'd made a mistake. Sex with Mel wouldn't be unpleasant, but . . . hell, he was starting to like the guy. He almost laughed at himself. You're

126

supposed to have sex with people you like . . .

He decided he'd have breakfast and make his next move. Maybe a jailhouse visit with Mel's former lover, Nick Brash. He was about to make a U-turn when he spotted a police car pulling into the parking lot of Mel's bar. Some instinct made him follow. He watched as he drove into the lot and saw the chubby cop who'd been outside Sandy's house hammer at the back door.

No response.

The cop tried again and, with an aggrieved air, turned around.

"Hey," the cop said.

Adrian got out of his car.

"You got any idea where this guy is?"

"Who, Mel?"

"Yeah."

"Have you tried his house?"

"Yup. And who are you?"

"Adrian, and your name, sir?"

"Name's Kinney. Officer Jack Kinney."

Adrian shook his hand. Over Kinney's shoulder, he caught movement at the half-shuttered window of the bar. Mel was in there, hiding.

"You a friend of this guy's?"

Kinney was annoying Adrian now.

"Yes."

"Any idea what he was up to last night?"

"Yes, actually, I do. He was with me."

"You?"

"At his house. His sister was there. She'll verify it."

"And how long were you there?"

"Until about three o'clock this morning."

Kinney's disappointment was obvious and acute. "You sure about that?"

"Yes, very sure. Why?"

"Then he couldn't have done it," Kinney muttered.

"Done . . . what?"

"The homicides."

Adrian was shocked. "Both the father and the little boy are dead?"

"Nope. Kiddie's in the hospital . . . but he was left for dead."

Adrian couldn't help the sharpness to his tone. "Then he's still alive."

"For now."

What a peculiar man. Adrian felt it necessary to assure Kinney that Mel couldn't have bumped off anybody.

"He was up all night with me, up until we heard the screaming."

"You could hear it?"

"I'm sure they heard it for miles." Adrian remembered the sound. His words came out in a rush. "It was horrible."

Kinney looked pissed when he rolled out of the parking lot. Adrian waited until the police car was back on the highway before he approached the back door.

Mel opened it, and the misery on his face tore at Adrian.

"It's okay, I'm here now," he said and stepped into the bar.

Mel was hysterical. "I can't believe it. You have no idea how many times I wanted to hurt that woman—"

Adrian took Mel in his arms and held him until the other man calmed.

"You didn't do it."

"I know I didn't . . . but they're . . . they're hounding my family. My sister just told me that Sandy had something on every single person in town!"

"She had something on you?"

"Something?" Mel propelled himself away from Adrian.

"She had everything. Look at this place, she's ruined me! She took all my money . . . she squeezed me and squeezed me."

"She squeezed a lot of people, Mel. The police are talking to everybody."

Mel collapsed against the bar. "I would never hurt a kid, but I fucking wanted to run her down with my car a million times."

"She's been arrested. She'll pay for her crimes now." Adrian kept his tone soft. He looked at the back bar counter and was stunned to see three bottles of pills.

"What the—"

"No. Don't touch those. They're my . . ."

Adrian pushed himself away from Mel and stepped behind the bar.

"What the fuck? You're gonna kill yourself? Over that bitch?"

"She's ruined me. I'm in foreclosure!"

"We'll fight our way out of this together," Adrian said. "But I need to know, what did she have on you?"

Mel's head fell on the bar. He began banging it. Hard.

Adrian grabbed his head, looking into the sobbing man's face.

"What did she have on you?"

"I can't tell you."

Adrian was shocked. It was the money. It had to be.

"I didn't want to do it. They made me. They tied me up and raped me."

"What?"

Mel's words came out in a scream. "Her husband taped the whole thing as a BDSM tape. Now do you understand? They're gonna think I killed him."

"And I know you didn't."

Adrian took the pills and hurled them down the sink. He ran around the bar, reaching for Mel, who sank into his arms.

There wasn't much to pack and, frankly, Knox was relieved to see the end of the freezing, strange little cabin. What really hurt was the knowledge that he couldn't stay with Rallus, as much as he wanted to. He had to go home and get Curtis. He had to get him and come back and find them both a room.

"I can't stay with you," he said, his voice coming out in a rasp.

"Why not?" Rallus leaned against the door, arms folded against his chest as if blocking Knox from leaving.

"My life is weird. My family is . . . evil. I have a dog."

"My family's deranged, my life is weird, and I love dogs."

"I—I have to go back to LA to get him. I miss him."

"So, we'll go together."

"No. If you meet them, you won't want me anymore."

"I love you, not your family."

Those three little words hung between them for a moment.

"You . . . love me?"

Rallus stepped toward him and pushed Knox to the bed. He sobbed as Rallus's tongue moved to his ear.

"What are you doing?" he asked.

There was no response, except for the impassioned licking that continued. Knox was thrown at first when Rallus starting licking the curve of his ear, inside and out, the incessant licking continued and, oddly, he found himself not only relaxing but becoming aware of different sensations as the licking grew intense, then feather-like. He felt the range of high excitement, sleepiness, erotic pleasure and a mounting hard-on all colliding into one another.

He lay there enjoying and receiving the impassioned joy

Rallus was giving him. He moaned as Rallus's hand moved to his fly, removed Knox's cock from its confines. For one brief moment, Rallus toyed with the leaking head, then removed his hand.

Knox almost cried out with frustration when Rallus took his hand away, and then something else took its place. Rallus's tongue started fucking his ear, like a long, slow cock, and Knox came so hard purple spots fused behind both eyes.

Mel lay on the bar floor, his tears falling in his ears. Adrian lay between his legs and kissed him, hard. The last time he'd been on this floor, three men had pinned him down as Steve DiNozza laughed and laughed, filming his degradation.

He could hardly believe he was naked and hard as Adrian's head dipped between his open thighs, his hot, sucking mouth working on his balls.

"Stroke your cock gently for me," Adrian said, dropping a kiss on Mel's inner thigh. "It will make your orgasm stronger. I'll stroke your ass as I suck your cock."

"Oh . . ." Mel's cries bounced off the walls.

"I love the way your ass bucks against my hand." Adrian dropped a kiss on Mel's cock. Oh man, the way that mouth came over the head. Mel fought the urge to come.

"It's been so long . . . so long. Your mouth is pure magic."

He felt Adrian's mouth bobbing on his cock, coming off it to lick at the juices leaking freely now. Adrian's finger moved into him. Once again, he came off Mel's cock for a second to lick Mel's balls. He found Mel's own fingers there and licked them, too.

As he moved back to Mel's cock, he slipped two fingers inside him, and Mel went crazy.

Adrian reached up and tweaked one of Mel's nipples, then the other. He sucked Mel's cock all the way into his throat, squeezing Mel's balls with his free hand.

Mel's ass shot into the air, and he humped Adrian's face as red, and blue lights flashed outside.

"Open up. It's the police!"

Rallus felt a great contentment and a ripple of fear as he loaded Knox's belongings into his truck and they headed back to his cabin. The two men held hands as they drove. The air was crisp and cool, the sky a spectacular blue. Snow on the ground looked dirty as they took the highway.

Old Mr. Gower was walking, pushing what looked like the baby doll in a baby buggy. He spied Rallus and Knox and lifted a hand in greeting.

"I think I know where Mr. Herxheimer went," Knox said, looking over his shoulder.

"Yeah." Rallus pulled into the driveway.

They unloaded Knox's gear, and there was a knock at the back door.

Half expecting Penny, he was surprised to see Detective Fisk.

"Detective. Wow, how did you find me?"

Fisk shrugged. "Small town."

Rallus said nothing. He didn't invite Fisk inside. He waited the cop out, and Fisk didn't waste a breath.

"I want to know how you figured Nick Brash was in danger? They just found him swinging in his cell."

Rallus took the news calmly.

"I'm a cop."

"No, you're not. You're a goddamn retired FBI field officer. You could have told me."

"You weren't interested in my help a couple of hours ago."

"That's before I knew who you were. What's this Rallus

nonsense, anyway?"

"The name I choose to go by now."

"How did you know about Brash?"

"I didn't know. I figured everything points back to him. I think he and Steve pulled the bank job, like I told you. Whoever put Steve out of business was likely to shut Brash up . . . permanently."

"Sandy DiNozza escaped custody," Fisk said.

"Now that does surprise me. How did she manage that?"

"Can you believe it?" Fisk shook his head.

"Did it happen at Lynwood jail?"

Fisk stared at him. "How do you do that?"

Rallus lifted his shoulders. "Not the first time it's happened, that a desperate detainee slips through the cracks."

Fisk blew out a breath. "She somehow got herself into the wrong line, and by the time they realized she was missing, she was gone."

"I hope there's an armed guard on Mikey's hospital room. She might be a bitch and a con artist, but I think she genuinely loves that kid."

Fisk nodded. "It's in place. Listen, I could use your help."

Rallus shook his head. "All the pieces are falling into place. You don't need me."

"Yes, I do."

"No. My life needs me. I—" Man . . . why is it so hard to admit this? "I don't know how much time I have."

"None of us do," Fisk said.

"No, you don't understand. I . . . I have limited time. I—" He looked over his shoulder. "I'm sorry. For once in my life, I'm thinking about me."

"But—"

Rallus walked back inside and shut the door on Detective Fisk.

"FBI," Knox mouthed. "You were FBI?"

He shrugged.

"What did you mean when you said—"

"Shush," Rallus said, pulling Knox into his arms. Then he started to tremble; Rallus had never trembled before. "That doesn't matter."

"I'm scared."

"No."

Knox pulled out of his embrace. "What's your real name?"

"Rallus."

"That's a lie. Why did you change your name?"

"Because I . . ." He swallowed. "Because I wanted to be someone else."

"Not an agent? Was it the job, something happened and . . ."

"No, it wasn't the job. It wasn't that I didn't want to be FBI, it was that I wanted to be another person . . . another person who didn't have . . ." He choked.

"Didn't have what? Didn't have what?" Knox insisted.

"I'm dying," he said softly. He heaved a sob, then his expression looked calm, unemotional.

"Dying?" The word stuck in his throat. "No."

He nodded. "I'm sorry. I should have told you, but I . . ." He shook his head, turned away. "I couldn't. Sex had always been for fun, and after I was diagnosed, I was determined to have a lot of it, with anyone I pleased. No commitments, hot sex and move on. But . . ." He turned and looked at him. "I wasn't counting on you."

Silent tears rolled down Knox's face. "There's no cure for . . . is it cancer?"

"Brain tumor."

He nodded silently.

"I was told it was inoperable. I have a year, maybe less." He cleared his throat. "No one knows, not even my family. If you want to leave now, I won't . . ."

"Leave?" Knox shook his head. "Why in the hell would I leave?" He came closer, reached out and touched his face. "What's your real name? Don't tell me if you—"

"Travis. My first name is Travis. Rallus is actually my middle name."

Knox drew him close to him. "I don't care how much time we have. I want to spend every minute with you. I love you."

Rallus buried his face in Knox's neck and left it there for a long time.

"I want to help you," Adrian announced. He was sitting on the edge of the bar, sipping a glass of wine.

Mel watched him as if hypnotized from where he still lay on the floor. He could hardly register what in hell he was saying. All he could do was look at him and wonder what angel had sent him.

"Did you hear me?"

"You want to help me with what?" He blinked.

"I want to invest in this place if you'll let me. Would you consider taking on a partner?"

"Partner, like business partner?"

"That be the one." He slipped off the bar.

"Hell yes," Mel got up off the floor. "But it would take a hell of a lot of money, can you . . . I mean, you're an architect and all but . . ."

"I'm not."

"You're not?"

Adrian sighed. "I was sent here to investigate you. I work for the insurance company."

"What?" Mel's heart sank. It had all been a scam, an act. He knew that it was too good to be true. He was too good to be true. "It was all a lie?"

Adrian came closer, placed a hand on his shoulder. Mel shook it off. "Get out. Don't touch me, get away from me."

"Listen," Adrian pleaded. "I never believed that you were guilty. If I had, I wouldn't have . . . Mel, I really care about you. What happened here just now was no act. I should have told you the truth but I couldn't. I'm off the case now. I'm calling the company tonight and resigning. I want to stay here with you, build this place up. Please, let me."

"Why?" Mel muttered bitterly. "Am I that pathetic that I need your pity?"

"No. I need you. It has nothing to do with pity. I think I may be falling in love. Give me a chance to find out. Please."

Mel picked up his clothes. "I need to be alone. Please, leave."

Adrian nodded. He placed his card on the bar. "Call me. I'll stay in town for a few days in case . . ."

"I won't."

"You won't do anything . . . I mean . . ."

"Don't worry, I won't kill myself. You won't have to live with that."

"Mel!"

Mel choked back a cry and left the room.

He was happy to see that Adrian had left by the time he reemerged. Today had been a dream, but it was over. He should just sell this place and get out while the going was good.

When a knock came on the door, he ran to it, thinking it was Adrian and . . . it wasn't. It was a cop. He flashed his badge and walked in. He didn't bother to sugarcoat his announcement. "Did you know that your ex hanged himself in his jail cell?"

Mel's jaw dropped.

Penny kept trying to get Mel to eat, but he had no appetite. It was true that Nick was an ass, but he didn't deserve that. No one did.

"Why now?" he asked his sister for the tenth time.

"I don't know. Maybe he was tired of living in prison. You shouldn't beat yourself up over it, Mel. It's not your fault."

In truth, it was Adrian he was beating himself up over. He missed him. Maybe he'd made a mistake. Maybe he'd been sincere about everything. Could he trust him? He had to start trusting someone again.

"Thanks, sis." He reached across the table and then stood. He took out the card Adrian had given him and went upstairs to his room. He picked up the phone and dialed.

"Mel?" Adrian answered as if he'd been waiting for his call.

"You weren't jiving me today, were you, when you said you—"

"No. I meant it. Come to me tonight, Mel, come to my hotel, and I'll prove it to you."

A little thrill went up Mel's spine. "I'll be right there," he said and hung up the phone.

"What's going on?" Penny sister asked as her brother came bounding down the stairs with his car keys dangling from his fist.

"I'm ah . . . going out," he said.

She eyed him. "With Adrian?"

He nodded.

"Are you sure?"

"I have to give it a shot. I have to get a life."

She hugged him. "You go, boy," she whispered.

He left with a smile on his face. She hadn't seen him do that a hell of a lot lately.

"Don't worry," a voice said from the other room, "he'll do fine with that Adrian fellow. He's sincere."

Penny narrowed her eyes. She saw a figure standing in the archway of the living room. "Dad?"

"Yes, my daughter."

He'd never called her "my daughter" in her life. "Are you alright?"

"I never felt better actually. Want to dance?"

Her eyes widened. "Dance?" A few months ago, he couldn't remember his own name, let alone remember how to dance.

He came out of the shadows, a beaming smile on his face. Gone was the blank stare that usually appeared on his face.

"Shouldn't you be asleep?"

"Asleep? What for? The night is young," he said. "So, now that your brother has someone to squeeze in the night, when are you going to find someone? It's time," he said, giving her a meaningful look.

She gasped as he suddenly reached out and pulled her up against him. "Waltz?"

CHAPTER NINE

No one was going to take her boy, lock him up in some institution and throw the key away. No one. She walked steadily down the corridor of the hospital. She knew right where he was. The guard was the big white flag that advertised his room number. She concentrated. Steve used to laugh at her. You're no psychic, don't have a psychic bone in your bone, you bitch. But she'd show him. She'd show them all.

She stopped in front of the guard and smiled. He was a big burly man with white hair. Before he could shoot any questions at her, she pierced him with her gaze.

You will let me by. You won't say a word.

The guard glanced at her. He looked dazed as he sat back down in the chair, staring straight ahead at something on the wall. She smiled and hurried into Michael's room. He was lying in the bed, his head turned to the side. It looked as if he'd been heavily sedated.

"What have they done to my boy? Don't worry now, sweetie, Mommy's here." She took down the blanket and carefully lifted him into her arms. "Mommy's big boy," she murmured, holding him close, kissing the top of his head. Quickly she hurried from the room and made her way to the exit stairs at the end of the corridor. She took the steps, two at a time, holding onto the rail with one hand and clutching Michael close to her chest with the other.

As they got outside, he began to whimper softly.

"Shush," she cooed, "Mama is here. No one is going to

hurt you." She rocked Michael back and forth in her arms, and spotting the taxi stand across the road, made a beeline for it, dodging the traffic as she skipped across the busy intersection. She wrenched open the door of the first taxi she came to and slid into the backseat.

"Where to, lady?" the cabbie inquired, glancing at her in his rearview.

"To the airport," she told him, "and there's one hundred dollars in it for you if you get me there in thirty minutes."

The driver roared the engine to life, and they were on their way.

Knox lay awake watching Rallus as he slept. He couldn't get used to calling him Travis. He'd always be Rallus to him. He breathed a sigh of relief each time he saw his chest rise and fall. It was hard to believe that he was ... Oh God, he couldn't even think the word, let alone say it. It scared the shit out of him. He couldn't lose him, not now when he'd discovered the joy of love for the first time in his life. It was too cruel, totally and utterly unfair. But then again, when had life ever promised to be fair.

The knock on the door startled him. Knox squinted at the alarm clock. It was barely four o'clock in the morning, the sun not yet risen in the sky. He looked at Rallus, hoping he wouldn't wake up. It was probably just some drunk at the wrong door.

"Um, who in the hell is that?" Rallus asked sleepily as the knock turned into pounding.

Knox was already out of bed, reaching for his pants. "No idea, probably just someone at the wrong door. I'll handle it. Go back to sleep, my love. Hold on," he muttered, approaching the door. "Who is it?"

"It's Detective Fisk. I got to talk to Travis Montana, now."

Knox opened the door. Montana. So that was his last name . . . Travis Rallus Montana. Sweet. "Do you have any idea what time it is? Rallus already told you that . . ."

Fisk pushed by him.

Rallus was already sitting up in bed. He ran a hand through his disarrayed dark hair and glared at Fisk. "This better be good."

Fisk picked up a shirt off the floor and threw it at him. "Get your clothes on, Romeo. That lunatic woman has stolen the kid right out of the hospital room. I need your help."

Rallus examined the shirt. "First of all, this isn't my shirt. Second of all, tell me again why this is my problem?"

"Because you care, and because you got a sixth sense for this shit," Fisk fired back. He looked tired, at the end of his rope.

Knox sank onto the bed. "I can't believe she'd do that. How? I thought there was a guard on the room?"

"She used mind control," Rallus said. "It only works for a few minutes, but it's effective if you have the sight."

"That's what the guard said. Needless to say, his boss said it was horseshit, and he'll be looking for a new job."

"It's not horseshit," Rallus shook his head.

"See, that's why I need you," Fisk threw up his hands. "So, she's some kind of a magician or what?"

Rallus swung his long legs over the bed. "She's not a magician," he replied calmly. "She's got the second sight. She probably just planted a suggestion in the mind of the guard." He began to dress. "I knew of this guy in Alaska once that had it. He pulled off a string of unarmed robberies just by planting a suggestion in the minds of the guards, even got them to turn off the alarm system for him. Took us a while to figure out that's how he did it."

"Then it's real."

"Oh yeah."

Knox studied Rallus as he did up his jeans. "Where do you think you're going? You're not going anywhere."

"Why in hell not, Mother?" He gave him a wide grin.

"Because you're . . ." He stopped. "I thought you said you wanted to take time for you and . . ."

"But there's something more important than me right now," he said softly, reaching over and touching Knox's shoulder with a meaningful look in his eyes.

"Bossy little bugger, isn't he?" Fisk smirked.

Knox clicked his tongue and shot the detective a dirty look. "I know that, but you'd think the police could handle this without you."

He shrugged. "Well, they need me. Knox, I can't let her just take that kid. He doesn't even belong to her, and what in hell kind of a life is he going to have with her? She's a criminal, and probably deranged to boot."

"Where do we start?" Fisk asked him, sounding impatient.

"The airport," Rallus told him, "and we better move our asses. Pick up your phone and alert the airport authorities to be on the lookout for woman with a small boy. And request permission for an Amber Alert. Have the department fax over some photographs. Caution them to think of any excuse to delay them without telling them why. If she gets suspicious, she'll be out of there, and we'll lose her again."

"I'm coming with you," Knox insisted.

"No, you stay here," Rallus replied, kissing him on the tip of the nose. "You got a dead guy to watch, remember, and don't let this get away. We don't even know where Harold is."

"Dead guy?" Fisk raised an eyebrow on the way to the door. "Who's Harold?"

"It's ah . . . a long story." Rallus smiled faintly. Don't worry, there's no foul play. The guy is already dead. Knox just has to watch him to make sure he doesn't go anywhere."

"How in the hell could he be going anywhere if he's dead?" Fisk demanded.

"You'd be surprised." Rallus grinned, looked over his shoulder at Knox, winked, and was out the door.

Knox sank down on the bed and picked absently at the blanket. What if something happened to Rallus when he was out there with Fisk? What if the exertion was too much for him? He got up and walked into the kitchen. He opened the cupboard and stared again at the multitudes of pill bottles all lined up in a row. Had he taken his medication? Knox took each bottle in his hand, one by one: Dexamethasone, prednisone, methylprednisolone.

He knew what these were. As a hustler, he'd sometimes swiped drugs from tricks . . . and he was paid by a couple of them to pick up their prescriptions. He made it his business to know what he was collecting. He wanted to know what he was going back to his tricks with. He took a deep breath, bothered by the memories. He was sadly familiar with all of these names. There were steroids designed to control seizures, anti-epileptic drugs, drugs for pain, drugs to fight insomnia, drugs that helped to ease the side effects of other drugs.

He opened the bottles, they seemed full. They'd been dispensed over a month ago. He hadn't been taking any of them. He sighed, closed the door. Why in hell wasn't he taking the medication?

Knox checked his watch. It was time to go to work. Time to watch the dead.

It was heaven waking up next to Adrian. Mel felt all warm and secure, cuddled in his arms, trying not to let that little voice inside of him make him crazy, that little voice that warned, Don't trust him. You know what happened the last time. Adrian was awake now, looking at him, smiling. "Hey, good morning."

"Good morning." Mel felt like he was blushing.

"So, did I prove my sincerity last night, or what? Do you believe me now?"

"You certainly made a stab at it," Mel joked.

Adrian laughed and pulled him in tighter against his body. "You better sound more convinced than that or I might tickle you until you do."

Mel laughed. "I'm not ticklish."

"Oh yeah." Adrian started to tickle him.

Mel laughed. "Okay, okay, stop."

Adrian sobered. "I'm anxious to get started. I think we should tear down that wall in between the pool tables and the stage, make it an open concept. We could add some dart boards, too. What do you think about mocha as a color?"

"Sounds great. Are we doing all this ourselves?"

"Cheaper that way. With a little elbow grease and muscle, we can whip that place into shape in no time. We need a live band, classic rock, something to bring in the crowd."

"And you got the muscle, baby." Mel growled and ran a hand over one of Adrian's firm, muscled biceps.

Adrian kissed him deeply on the mouth. "Are you good with paint?"

"Body paint, if it's your body. I'd enjoy painting your naked hide."

"Get serious. You know what I mean."

"Well, aren't you all serious this early in the morning," Mel mocked and dipped his head under the blanket.

Adrian protested but then made a sound of pleasure in his throat as Mel began to lick his cock. "That's nice. Very nice. Keep going."

"I want to suck it. Can I, or would you rather discuss

paint?"

"Smartass." He grunted, pressing Mel's head down between his legs. "If you're gooood . . . .ooh . . . okay, um, you can have it. Take it, boy."

Mel licked the underside of Adrian's cock and then the top of his shaft, swirling his tongue around the tip and then swallowing the head.

Adrian let out some air and relaxed back onto the pillow, pumping his hips gently upward into Mel's worshipping mouth. "We can discuss . . . ah . . . paint later . . ."

Fisk drove at breakneck speed in the direction of the airport. Rallus sat with his head to the side, his eyes closed. The headaches were always worse in the morning. Usually, they subsided by noon. This one made his head feel as if it were coming off his shoulders. He popped a couple of aspirin knowing they wouldn't help, but it made him feel better about the headache for some reason. He'd stopped taking the medication because the side effects were very bad. First of all, he couldn't get an erection worth shit, and his face would bloat, his vision blur. No, if he was going to die, he wasn't going to die as some bloated old impotent invalid.

"Did you alert the airport?" Rallus asked suddenly, pretty sure that Fisk had already done that.

"You heard me on the phone."

"Yeah." He had, of course, just didn't remember. He needed coffee or something.

The airport was coming into view on the left-hand side.

"Think she's still there?" Fisk asked.

"I doubt it," Rallus murmured. "Knowing airport security, they tipped her off. Probably announced that she was wanted over the loudspeaker."

"Hey," Fisk laughed, "you're a pretty funny guy."

"Yeah, I'm a laugh riot," he said, rubbing his temples.

"Got a headache?"

"Wouldn't believe it if I told you."

"I heard about you, you know."

"Oh yeah, what did you hear?"

"That you were the best field officer the bureau had. And that you lived your job."

"Yeah, I lived it." He'd lived it all right, and he was paying for it. Lack of sleep, improper eating habits, excessive stress, all of those things he knew had helped bring him to this place where he lingered between the abyss of life and death. "Walk the line," he murmured.

"What?"

"Nothing." He laughed out loud.

Fisk sped up in front of the airport, ignoring the protests of the security guard. He flashed his badge and headed to the entrance. Rallus was at his heels. When he looked down, the pavement began to weave in and out. When he looked up, his vision blurred, and he felt dizzy, a little nauseous. Hold on. Get her, and find Michael, then you can act like a guy with a terminal disease.

Fisk was talking to, or rather bellowing at, the security man in charge. He wasn't going to get anywhere that way. Rallus elbowed past him. "Listen, have you seen anyone fitting that description"—he pointed at the photo the man had in front of him—"with a small boy of around six?"

"I've checked the computer, no one of that name . . ."

"Of course not, you idiot," Fisk barked, "she's not going to use her real name for Christ's sakes."

"Fisk," Rallus touched his arm, he knew the guy was on the border of exhaustion, he'd been there, "go get a coffee."

Fisk muttered something and walked off.

"I want all main exits manned. No one leaves here unless they are checked first, and all female passengers traveling with a six-year-old are to be detained. Is that clear?"

He nodded, swallowing hard.

"All security personnel should have a picture and description of the suspect, all exits watched. Now, open up your departure files, and bring up any female passenger traveling with a child of six years. Dispatch to all planes which have left the ground in the last two hours a description of the suspect. I want all passengers verified and identified. "

"It would take me a while to isolate those statistics."

"Just do it." Rallus looked around. The airport seemed to spin for a few minutes, then stabilize. "I'll find you, honey," he said under his breath. "You won't get away."

"Well, Mr. Mandelstamm," Knox said, walking around the body and checking to see that all candles were lit, "looks like this is your last night with us. I'll be leaving, too. I'm going to get my dog, then I don't know really what's going to happen. I'm scared."

Mr. Mandelstamm politely listened to his conversation. After all, there wasn't much else he could do, was there?

Knox settled back on the sofa, his unopened book at his side. He hoped that Michael was safe. He hoped that Rallus was safe. He hadn't heard anything from him, and it was almost evening. Had they found the boy? And what about Harold? He'd no idea where he'd ended up, or if his spirit had really been responsible for that murder or not. It would be good to get out of this town.

He closed his eyes. "Rallus, I love you," he said aloud.

A single tear ran down his face, and he brushed it away hastily. "Well, Mr. Mandelstamm, maybe I can call you Benjamin now, I feel as if we know each other well enough to be on a first name basis. It's just you and me, how about some

Harry Potter?"

Mel looked at Adrian in horror when he picked up the axe and chopped into the wall. It wasn't as if he didn't know what the plan was, it was just shocking to see it being carried out.

As if sensing his trepidation, Adrian paused and gave Mel a sympathetic look. "It's okay, honey, I tell you, it will be great when it's finished."

"Are you sure you know what you're doing?"

"Kind of," he teased.

"Kind of?"

He chuckled. "Come on. Give me a hand will you? Pick up that crowbar. Let's get this wall down."

The wall came down rather quickly with the two of them hammering away at it. Mel was elated when he found himself staring through to the other room.

"Adrian, this is fantastic." He paused when he heard only silence. "Adrian?"

He glanced down at the floor to where Adrian was kneeling, his hand holding something which looked like a bundle of papers.

"What's that?" Mel asked, walking over to where he knelt.

Adrian looked up at him, then back down at the package. Mel's eyes widened when he saw what he was holding. "Oh my God," Mel muttered. "It's . . . it's . . ."

"Yeah, money, lots and lots of money."

She was trapped, trapped before she even got off the ground. Even the bathrooms weren't safe. She hid in one after another, knowing that soon they'd get around the searching the one she was in, again. She didn't make her flight to Mexico. In fact, she heard it announced, and then stared miserably at her watch, knowing that it was leaving the ground.

Michael was awake but lethargic, and he was hungry. He'd been crying for the last hour.

"Fuck, fuck, fuck," she muttered.

She couldn't get out the exits, and she couldn't get on a plane. If she even tried to make it to the exit where maybe she could plant a suggestion in the mind of the guard, they'd see her on the cameras. No, she'd just have to wait it out until she could think of something, but where could she hide?

Slowly, she exited the woman's bathroom and hurried along the hallway with her head down. In the distance, she could see Rallus. He was leaning against one of the information counters. He didn't look so hot, but she wasn't about to let that fool her. She knew if anyone caught her, he would. And then she knew what she had to do. She leaned against the wall and focused on him. Even at this distance, she could probably get him to come to her. You want me, I'm here. Alert no one. Come now.

He picked up his head, but he didn't move.

What in hell . . . She tried again. Nothing. Was he immune? She focused harder, then she saw it. It blocked her abilities, solid and deadly. He was dying. She felt a momentary rush of sadness, if only because he was so damn good-looking. What was he doing here? He should be in a hospital. She'd have to forget about using him. There was that buffoon of a detective. He was standing beside the younger man now. Come, Detective. I have something for you.

Fisk took a step in her direction. Rallus placed a hand on his arm, held him back.

"Damn you," she muttered. "How did you know?"

"Turn around slowly," a gruff voice said. She heard the

click of artillery. She smiled, slowly turning.

"I can't put up my hands. I have the boy."

"Put the boy down," the man in army fatigues said.

"I think not." She smiled. "My, I must be important, what with all you uniformed men in tow."

A hand settled on her shoulder now. She jumped, turned around.

"It's all over," Rallus said.

"You told them to come up behind me, didn't you?"

"Give me the baby," he said.

She shook her head. "He's the only protection I have. I'm sorry about the tumor, really."

He raised an eyebrow.

"You're not susceptible to my mind control," she commented, holding Michael closer. He started to cry.

That man was looking at her. Was it compassion he saw in his eyes? She wasn't sure.

"If you love him, give him a chance, Sandy. He's not yours."

"His mother was a crackhead, Rallus, a crackhead. Am I worse?"

"You love him enough to give him to me. So, do it. If you do, they won't shoot you."

"And I'll rot in prison, right?"

He didn't reply. "Give me the boy."

She looked at him. "You have a few minutes," she told him, then tossed him the boy and threw her hands in the air. "I have a gun," she screamed and began to run.

Rallus reared back, the boy in his arms. Two shots rang out, and she was facedown on the floor, blood pooling around her head.

The little boy stopped crying suddenly. He placed his head on Rallus shoulder, and then Rallus felt himself waver. "Take him," he told one of the soldiers nearby. "Take him now." He was conscious of the boy leaving his arms, then he went to his knees, his body convulsing violently then blackness.

Four hours later, Knox sat in the hospital waiting room. Detective Fisk handed him his third cup of shitty coffee. "He's a hero. He really saved the day. I'm sure that we would have lost her if it hadn't been for Montana."

Knox nodded. He appreciated what he was saying. He was happy that Michael was alive and well, and would now have a chance at a better life, but all he could think about was Rallus, and the fact that he could be losing him.

Two hours and there was no news.

"They may have to move him. This hospital isn't equipped for . . . I had no idea he had a brain tumor," Fisk cleared his throat.

"Well, he didn't want people to know." Knox put his face in his hands. Maybe if he'd taken his medication. Maybe if he'd stayed in bed today and . . ."He's going to die, isn't he?"

"I don't know. Maybe not. He had a convulsion or something and then he was out. I've never seen anything like it. He had a headache this morning, at least that's what he said, but he's not a big complainer."

"No," Knox muttered. "He's a strong, brave man, maybe too much so . . . to his own detriment."

When the doctor came down the hall, Knox jumped to his feet. He waited until the doctor was standing in front of him. He could scarcely breathe. The look on the doctor's face didn't look optimistic. "I'm sorry. He's in a coma. I doubt that he'll come out of it."

Knox lowered his head and sobbed.

The doctor placed a hand on his shoulder. "You can sit

with him if you like."

Knox wiped his tears.

Fisk patted his back. "I'm sorry, kid. I gotta go, but I'll be back, okay?"

"Thanks." Knox watched the detective go, then walked into the bathroom to wash his face, and try to pull himself together. He looked up as the door opened. A face glanced back at him through the mirror. It was a wrinkled one, topped with snow-white hair. He knew that face. He turned around.

"Mr. Gower? Can I help you with something? Is Penny outside? It was really nice of her to come."

"I came alone."

"Alone?"

"Yes. I came to talk to you, Knox."

The voice sounded strange like it didn't belong to Mr. Gower at all. And besides, Penny's father was in a wheel-chair and senile. "Who are you?"

"You know who I am."

"Harold? Oh, my God."

"We need each other, Knox. Don't think of leaving Fawn-skin."

"You can't force me to stay here."

"You started this. You will help me finish it."

"Finish what? Damn it, don't you realize this is not the time? I'm losing him."

"I can fix that."

"What?"

"I can bring him back. What is he worth to you?"

"He's worth everything to me." He reached out and clutched the man's arm. "What do I have to do?"

"Stay. That's all. Just stay until it's over."

"Until what's over?"

"I can't tell you that."

"Can you cure him, take it away?"

"No, but I can keep him away from the pull of death."

"It's enough." Knox nodded.

He pointed at him. "Don't betray me, or I swear, I'll take him with me when I go. Do you understand?"

Knox opened his mouth to say something, but he found himself suddenly alone. A cold shiver ran up his spine.

Knox remained in the bathroom for a few more minutes, his hands shaking, then he pushed open the door and raced down the hallway to the room where Rallus was lying, hooked up to a variety of machines. He didn't think about what had just happened in the bathroom. Rallus filled his mind and his heart, blotting out everything else. Knox touched his cheek. He was still, his skin cool to touch.

"Rallus," he whispered softly, "I love you. Come back to me, baby."

Rallus's eyes fluttered open. "Knox?" he murmured, "where am I?"

Knox stared at him stunned. Grateful tears fell down his face as he leaned over and kissed Rallus tenderly on the mouth.

Harold had really done this. He'd brought Rallus back to him.

YOU MAY ALSO ENJOY THE FOLLOWING FROM EXTASY BOOKS INC:

Frenzied
A.J. Llewellyn and D.J. Manly

Excerpt

Mrs. King bashed on Rallus's door. She was so worked up, certain that the two men were ignoring her, that she was still knocking when Rallus answered.

She fell inside the door, stumbling over the top step. He caught her in his arms.

"I have to talk to you about Mrs. Schmuckler," she said, smoothing down her tight woolen skirt.

Rallus straightened her, giving her an odd look.

"Who?"

"Mrs. Schmuckler."

She brushed past him and pounced on Knox, who was sitting at the dining room table, eating muffins.

"Why haven't you been to see me? You know I need your help. I've called you so many times, I—"

"We're in the middle of something here," Rallus said.

She squinted at him. "What?"

"I'm not at liberty to say."

"But—"

"What time do you need Knox there? We'll both come."

"Really?" Her cheeks reddened, she could feel it. "I—"

Penny's cell phone rang. Mrs. King realized in that moment that there were two cops in the room besides Penny.

"What's going on?" she asked.

"You need to leave now. What time do you want us there?" Rallus steered her back toward the door.

"Eight." He held the door open and gave her a little shove. She almost fell down the stairs.

Well, really! She could have sworn she heard Penny say the name Sandy. But it couldn't be. She walked back to the funeral home. Okay, so she'd have to wait several more hours. She was sure her clients would be impressed that a retired FBI agent was going to sit with the dead.

I can't afford another slip-up like the one we had with Harold.

She opened her front door and yelped at the sudden sensation of icy fingers goosing her. She heard crazy laughter in her ear.

"Harold?" she hissed, glancing around fearfully. She was terrified of Harold materializing before her. She wasn't into ghosts. In spite of her profession, she had no desire to see dead people.

Some of the bereaved family members standing in small groups in her hallway turned and stared at her. She smiled back, pushing back blonde tendrils of hair that had escaped her one-hundred dollar hairdo.

"Good news!" Mrs. King stepped forward, taking the hands of Mrs. Schmuckler's daughter, Evelyn. "I have the perfect shomerim for you tonight!"

She heard a mad, defiant cackle that stopped the soft murmurings of the mourners for a moment.

"It's the wind," she said. She was smiling in the insincere way her son said made her face look like a tomahawk. She tried to tame it. "These draughty old houses really pick up the wind."

The icy fingers grabbed a good bit of her bottom this time and pinched. Mrs. King yelped. She had the nasty sensation of a tongue poking in her ear. She pawed at it and thought she would pass out when she felt the tongue at her other ear.

God help me . . . we need an exorcist.

She picked up a tray of cookies, hoping nobody would notice her shaky hands.

The iciness invaded her whole body.

One of the grieving women plucked a cookie from the proffered tray.

"Dershtikt zolstu veren!" Mrs. King felt the words tumble from her mouth involuntarily and heard the collective gasps.

"What did I say? What did I say?" she asked, mortified.

One of the men pointed a shaky finger at her.

"You just told her she should choke on it!"

"Oh, my God!"

Mrs. King stared at him. She felt the alien spirit in her, warring with her better nature. She steeled herself against further interference.

Wait until I get my hands on Knox . . . it's his fault Harold is doing this to me!

She smiled with all the dignity and self-possession she could muster.

"I should have known better than to try and learn Yiddish expressions on the Internet."

Her sympathetic smile must have worked. Some of the mourners softened. A few angry faces still stared at her.

Help me, Harold screamed in her head. *Help me, or I'll make worse trouble for you!*

ABOUT THE AUTHORS

A.J. Llewellyn divides her time between California and Hawaii. Bags of Kona coffee in the fridge and a healthy collection of Hawaiian records keep her refueled when she is on the mainland. A.J.'s passion for the islands led her to writing a play about the last ruling monarch of Hawaii, Queen Lili'uokalani. She has written a non-erotic novel about the overthrow of her kingdom—in diary form from her maid's point of view.

She never lacks inspiration for male/male erotic romances and has to force her fingers from the computer keyboard to pursue other passions: collecting books on Hawaiiana, surfing and spending time with her family, friends and animal companions.

A.J. Llewellyn believes that love is a song best sung out loud. To find out more about A.J., visit her website at http://www.ajllewellyn.com or you can reach her at aj@ajllewellyn.com.

D.J. Manly says, "I write not only for my own pleasure, but for the pleasure of my readers. I can't remember a time in my life when I haven't written and told stories. When I'm not writing, I'm dreaming about writing, doing something wild and adventurous, or trying to make the world a better and more open-minded place to live in. I adore beautiful men, and I know I'm not alone in this! Eroticism between consenting adults, in all its many forms, is the icing on the cake of life!"

www.ingramcontent.com/pod-product-compliance
Lightning Source LLC
Chambersburg PA
CBHW060825120626
46557CB00001B/368